The Way I See It

Series by LB Tillit

Ozzie-Book 1

Zonta-Book 2

Zonta

L.B. Tillit

Dedication

To all who try to do what is right, yet still feel alone and afraid. And to those who dare to step up and walk beside them.

Chapter 1
Carlos

what r u doing rn

I froze as I looked at the text. It was from Carlos. How did he get my number? The guy was a total creep and wouldn't leave me alone at school. I didn't want to respond. I didn't want him to know what I was doing. Ever! Still, I had to say something. I sat down on one of the plastic bins full of decorations.

hw

I lied. I was trying to set up for my Christmas party, but there was no way I was telling him that. It was almost four and I wasn't close to ready yet. I wondered who would even show up. The party wasn't supposed to start until six, so I should have been chill about it. But I wasn't. Even though I had left school early to get ready, I felt like everything was moving at a slow pace. The last thing I needed was to be distracted by Carlos.

r u trying to get rid of me? nw u doing hw

I growled at myself. Why did I give him such a lame answer? We had just started our winter break. I had to make him think I was joking since I didn't want to upset Carlos. If I kept it light, then maybe he would leave me alone.

jk

lol

Was I suddenly having a real conversation with a guy I never spoke to at school? I had to stop this soon. But before I could think of a way out, I felt my phone vibrate again.

since u don't have a bf how abt u and me hook up

My mouth dropped open. Ew! Should I text *ew*? Could I tell him he was the last person at school I would ever want to hook up with?

no thnxs

The response was too weak. There was so much more I meant to say. But I didn't want to make him mad. I had learned it was best *never* to make anyone mad if you could help it.

lol

Had he been joking? Was he just messing with me? But before I could come up with another text, he added one more.

send me a pic so I can rmbr u during break

There was no way I was sending him any sort of pic of me.

nw

cmon plz

I stared at the cream-colored walls and the gray wall-to-wall carpet. White throw pillows cluttered two brown leather couches that faced a huge flat-screen TV. My basement still looked like my basement and not a party. Except there was a fake Christmas tree in the far corner still waiting for ornaments. And, in the middle of the room, four strands of red tinsel snaked up the four concrete pillars that held up the rest of the house. I still had so much to do! But I felt stuck. How should I respond to Carlos? What would get him to leave me alone? There was no way I was going to give him what he wanted. But I had to figure out how to end this on a good note. Always a good note.

I had an idea. I took a pic of the back of my left hand and sent it. Maybe he would get the hint that I was done.

lol

got 2 go

I hoped that ended it, but he shot me one more text.

c u and that hot hand soon

I didn't respond. It could go on and on. But maybe he was done too? After a few minutes with no more texts, I felt my shoulders relax. But then I looked at the picture I took of my hand and frowned. I hoped he didn't think I was playing with him. I hoped he got the hint to leave me alone. But my stomach began to hurt. I was kidding myself if I thought it was that easy.

Chapter 2

Nice

I was sick of being nice. Or at least trying to be nice and kind and saying the right things to people. Even during that stupid text between Carlos and me, I was trying to be nice. What was wrong with me? My parents had taught me to be that good girl. But I was getting tired of it. Fast!

"LILLY AND OZZIE ARE HERE!" Mom yelled down the basement steps.

I jumped up and shoved my phone into my pocket. "OKAY. CAN YOU TELL THEM TO COME ON DOWN?" I yelled back. I reached into the plastic bin I had been sitting on and filled my arms full of plastic snowflakes attached to strings. I had to figure out where to hang them.

The only real sign that I was about to have a party was the pile of snack food and drinks. I had dumped them onto a plastic fold-out table next to the lame tree.

But I couldn't focus. I wanted to blame it on my ADHD, like always. An excuse that had worked for me over the years. And, more often than not, had been the real reason when I couldn't focus or was confused. But, at that moment, the truth was that Carlos was to blame. He'd messed up any last drop of me thinking clearly. I was close to just giving up.

Suddenly I had an idea. I dropped the snowflake strand on the carpet and pulled out my phone to text the one person who always made me feel better. Vonny. My best friend.

wish u were here helping me

I missed Vonny like crazy. She and I had always done everything together since we were little. Then her dad was chosen for some research project and took the whole Kumar family with him to travel in an RV for the year.

me 2!

Vonny's text made me smile. She had been excited at first about the trip. But after five months in the RV with her parents and younger brother and sister, she felt a need to be back in Hancock.

I wanted to tell her about Carlos and the stupid pic I sent, but that would have to wait for later. I had to focus on the party.

not sure y im having a party

y not have a party?

not as good w/ others as u r

not true

true

not

tell me who u would invite

Vonny listed a bunch of people that she knew well, but I only hung out with when she was around. I knew how to be nice to them, but I never could get past that level. Not like with Vonny. But I was always fine with it. Her group of friends was a good enough choice for me. I didn't have to figure out who I could trust or not. As long as Vonny was fine with them, then so was I. But with her gone, it had hit me hard that I was *not* really part of the group. At all.

your friends not mine

poor u. shut up and have a good time. u so need to chill out about this

I sent her a smiley face emoji. Although I didn't feel like smiling.

"Great basement!" Ozzie Waxman's voice pulled me away from my phone. He was slowly moving down the stairs wearing his favorite Cleveland Browns cap. Ozzie used one hand to grasp the iron railing that snaked along the wall, while he paid close attention to his right knee. A fancy knee brace hugged his leg. He clearly was not used to putting full weight on his leg yet. I hoped his massive size wouldn't bend the iron railing, since it was meant to be for show rather than for use. I suddenly felt guilty for thinking about the stupid railing, when I should be worrying about Ozzie making it safely down the stairs with his torn ACL. And then there was the fact that it had only been a little over two weeks since he scared the hell out of us. We thought he was going to kill himself. What was that all about? Didn't make any sense!

"Zonta?" Ozzie's voice drew me back from my run-away thoughts.

I quickly smiled. "Sorry . . . I mean . . . thanks!" I looked down at my phone.

"Who you texting?" Ozzie asked. My eyes went wide. Could he tell I was upset about Carlos? But then Ozzie added, "Is it Vonny?" I relaxed. Yes, he was right. It *was* Vonny he had caught me texting, not Carlos. That would have been bad since Ozzie was the boyfriend that Carlos was talking about. Even if we weren't dating anymore.

"Yeah. Hang on a sec." I quickly texted Vonny that I had to go, and then shoved my phone in the back pocket of my jeans. I picked up the snowflake strand off the floor and, with a frown, looked past Ozzie. "Where's Lilly?" I needed to focus on something else. Anything else.

Chapter 3

Not Okay

Ozzie turned his head to look back up the stairs. "Lilly said she had to run to her room first." He looked back at me and then at the empty room. He shifted awkwardly. "Is it okay I came on down? Or do you want me to wait upstairs?"

I felt my cheeks grow warm. How could I be so stupid and rude? "No, Ozzie, it's okay. Come . . . sit on the couch." I flung one arm out and pointed at the leather couches. "Pick one."

"Are you sure? You don't seem so sure." Ozzie began to move toward the couches. Each step was carefully planned. I could tell he wanted to get off his injured leg. I felt awful that he thought I didn't want to be around him . . . alone. But he *had* let the false rumor spread that we hooked up and then he dumped me. So even though he had cleared it up and told me he was sorry, I could see why he didn't want anyone to think that. Ever again. I guess I was a little happy that he still felt badly. On the other hand, I didn't want him to be weird all the time. I wanted him to feel at ease.

There it was. I was trained well. I had to be nice. I hated myself for not just shutting Carlos down. But Ozzie was *not* Carlos. I had to get that straight in my head. So this meant I needed to make sure Ozzie felt welcome.

I decided to walk next to him, still holding the stupid snowflakes. One long strand trailed behind me like a tail. "Yes. I am sure. I was just wondering where Lilly was because . . ." I didn't know how to explain it. Lilly had been living at our house for exactly 7 weeks and 1 day. I could have probably counted the hours, but that would have been silly. I was happy that she had called me to come get her the night her aunt's no-good boyfriend beat the crap out of her. I was shocked that she had actually held onto my number. I had given it to her when she first came to Hancock High. I was trying to be nice to the new girl, but she had never called me. Not until that night when I picked her up from a gas station on 17th Street. We took her in and gave her a place to stay. But I thought she would go back to her aunt's by now. I thought for sure her aunt would have knocked on our door and begged Lilly to come back and told her all about how she'd kicked the abusive boyfriend out the door. But no, that had *not* happened.

Lilly had made herself comfortable in our guest room. *Her* room. My black ankle boots that I let her borrow were ruined and my blue sweater and white tank were permanently stretched to fit her. Three weeks ago, Mom told me to get over myself and be nice, so I tried. When Mom walked out of my room carrying all the clothes I hadn't worn in years, I told her it was fine. They were snug on Lilly, but she didn't care. Mom threw in her own favorite blue winter coat, which looked great on Lilly. But it ticked me off last week when Dad came home from work and had bought Lilly a brand-new, red wool cap. Was she staying with us forever?

"Zonta? Are you okay?" Ozzie's voice pulled me away from my thoughts, again.

I wasn't okay, but I wasn't going to tell him. I wasn't going to tell anyone.

Chapter 4

Lilly

"Zonta!" Ozzie's voice was louder. "Are you okay? You *are* acting weird."

I smiled awkwardly. "I'm sorry. Yes, I'm okay." I looked toward the stairs. "It's only that I expected Lilly to help me out some." I began to move toward one of the walls as I picked up the trailing end of the plastic snowflake strand. "I'm so behind with getting ready for the party. I could use some help."

"She said she'd be right down." Ozzie suddenly sounded upbeat. He must have believed my explanation. He lifted his right leg up on the couch and shoved two of the throw pillows under it.

Without thinking, I said, "I guess you and Lilly are good friends now." Instantly, I regretted it. I quickly turned my back to him as I tied one end of the snowflake strand to an old nail sticking out of the wall. I didn't dare look at his reaction to my statement as I pulled the snowflakes across the room.

Ozzie's voice was still upbeat. "Yeah, she is a pretty good friend." He didn't say anything else as I looped the snowflakes around one of the pillars and then tightened the other end of the snowflake strand to a hook on the opposite wall.

"Good!" I said too brightly as I turned around. But Ozzie was frowning at me. "What?" I asked.

"Something's wrong," Ozzie stated. He thought for a second before he added, "She's *not* my girlfriend."

I shifted awkwardly. "Nothing is wrong. *And* I don't care if she's your girlfriend or not." I meant it.

I heard my old ankle boots running down the stairs before I saw them. Lilly's face suddenly appeared. "Did I miss anything?" She smiled. Her wild green eyes lit up like the rest of her outfit.

Ozzie laughed at her over-the-top-ugly Christmas sweater. Flashing red and white lights covered a long green sweater. She looked like a living Christmas tree. I'd seen that outfit worn by Mom years ago to a party. Ozzie pointed to the opposite corner of the basement. "Zonta, it looks like you don't need to decorate your tree after all. Lilly can just stand in the corner."

I couldn't help but laugh, at least a little, as Lilly walked over to the corner and gave us her best Christmas tree poses. I had to remember that Lilly could be funny and chill. Mom had convinced Lilly to let her cut her hair and add blond highlights. Lilly's hair and white skin shone bright enough to look like a star on top of her tree-sweater. As soon as Lilly stopped trying to hook ornaments to her sweater, she looked around the room and her face became serious. "Is this all that you've done?"

"I can't do it by myself," I snapped. I growled at myself. I didn't want to be ugly to Lilly. She really hadn't done anything wrong. "I'm sorry. I just—"

"No, you sure can't!" Lilly stopped me and laughed as she unwrapped my snow-flake strand. "You'll behead someone with this!" She then wrapped the snowflakes around the Christmas tree, along with some flashing lights. "There! Tree is done! What's next?"

Chapter 5

Party

"Who did you invite?" Lilly asked as she stacked the now-cold pizzas. It was seven and no one had shown up yet. Ozzie and Lilly had pointed out that we really didn't need to decorate any more. We weren't ten years old and all anyone really cared about was food and music. So I had used Mom's credit card and ordered twelve Pizzas. We had even streamed music and dimmed the lights.

"Just a few people and I told them to bring their friends." I answered but realized my plan may have been a bad one. I felt stupid that I had been in a rush to run upstairs and change into my new black jeans, and my comfy-but-cute white sweater.

Ozzie laughed. "Really? Like who? Must be some great friends you have who will invite people for you."

I frowned, feeling stupid. I had even tamed my hair with gel so that it fell in perfect ringlets just below my shoulders. "Well . . . I invited some popular kids from school and thought they'd show up." After all, I had been voted on to the homecoming court just two months ago.

Didn't that mean I was popular? I grabbed my phone to look at my last post. "I also posted that I was having a party and everyone was welcome to come." Wouldn't everyone who voted for me want to come? My stomach flipped when I saw I only had two likes. But then I felt relief too. What if Carlos had seen the post? He would have shown up. As much as I wanted people to show up, I *didn't* want him. Even if he was some great football jock. I really hadn't thought any of it through. But I didn't know that Carlos really liked me and wanted more from me until a few hours earlier. At school, he *and* his friends harassed me all the time. They always looked me up and down like I was some tasty dessert. I ignored them, but they still scared me. Maybe it was good the party was a dud.

"Well, don't worry." Lilly smiled and rested her hand on the tower of cardboard boxes with *Hancock Pizza* printed in bold, black letters across the top. "It means more leftover pizza for us."

"Helloooo, anybody there?" someone yelled.

"Who's that?" Lilly asked as we all faced the stairs. I was shocked when Silvia Hemby came down the steps. She was a senior and had been Hancock High's Homecoming Queen. She lived in the Bence neighborhood with me. To be exact, the Hembys lived across the street from us in a huge, fancy house. Silvia and I used to hang together as kids, the way it is with most kids who live on the same street.

"Well, are you going to say hi?" Silvia asked as I stared at her, still shocked. She was also biracial, like me. Only difference was that her dad was black and her mom white. Problem was that my black mom and white dad thought that it made us close friends. But really, it only meant that she was a nice person and was kind to my parents. So she showed up with her mom and dad to all the events my parents hosted. Usually, we ended up in the basement, each on our own phones.

"Hi, Silvia," I grinned. I had hoped that a Christmas party that I planned would be different and that she'd come and bring some good friends. "Happy you could make it." At that moment I forgot about Carlos. I was so happy that it looked like my plan might work after all.

"Yeah, me too." Silvia pointed toward the stairs where a set of very high heels tried to slowly move down each step. "Brought a friend. Like you asked."

My smile dropped as I watched Chastity Shaw come into view. Silvia had to be kidding!

Chapter 6

A Sure Thing

I couldn't believe Silvia was friends with Chastity, since they were total opposites. I didn't know Chastity well, but she seemed slutty since she was always in one boy's lap or another. Her long, wavy brown hair and light green eyes stood out against her pale, white skin. It looked like she skipped her usually-heavy make-up and settled for two red streaks across her cheek bones.

"Aww, I like your tree," Chastity said too sweetly as she reached the bottom of the steps and headed for the food table. After she grabbed a bag of chips, she moved toward the couches to settle herself next to Ozzie. Ozzie shifted the throw pillows to keep her from sliding in too close.

"Thanks!" Lilly's voice boomed over the music. "The tree was my idea." Lilly moved quickly to stand behind Ozzie's couch.

Chastity looked Lilly up and down with disgust. "Who are you?"

Ozzie jumped in. "This is Lilly. You know, new to our school this year."

Chastity smiled at Ozzie and touched his knee brace. "No, I don't know. She looks like a tree and I don't talk to trees. But I know you." She tried to scoot in closer, and even reached out to grab his Brown's cap, but Ozzie's massive size and wall of pillows didn't let her move more than an inch.

"Okay, Chastity. Go find another football player." Ozzie was not happy.

"How about me?" A male voice boomed from the stairs. Owen Hemby was grinning as he took in the scene. "I thought this would be a lame party, but I see Chastity is here. My lucky day!" I rolled my eyes. Silvia must have invited him too. This was good, right? Panic set in. It was not good if she had invited the whole football team. Owen usually left me alone. He was only interested in the sure-thing girl. But he wasn't the one I was worried about.

"You didn't invite Carlos, did you?" I found myself as close to Silvia as I could get without biting the other end of the pizza slice that was half-way in her mouth.

Silvia didn't step back from me as she chewed and mumbled, "I didn't invite that jerk because he didn't come to my last party. He went to some other party instead of mine. Anyways, Owen is a distant cousin, so it was no big deal to invite him without the rest of the team." What party had Silvia had lately? I brushed the thought away, because she *always* had people over and I *always* wished I was a closer friend so she'd include me. I turned my head and saw Chastity and Owen take over the second couch as quickly as possible. Owen's red hair was almost the only thing visible as Chastity straddled him. Silvia laughed at the look of disgust on my face. "I know. Not really great company, but I promised Chastity and Owen I'd find a way to get them alone."

"They aren't exactly alone." I pointed out the obvious. Lilly returned to the back of the room to check out the snacks and Ozzie stood up from his couch to carefully walk over and join her.

Silvia looked at the huge basement and shrugged. "Well, they *are* *almost* alone." She took another bite of pizza before she saw I wasn't going anywhere. "Okay, okay. I'll get them to stop." Silvia walked over to the tangled couple who were starting to make noises. I thought I would throw up. "That's enough, love birds. Let's go."

"But I just got here!" Owen whined.

Chastity added, "You promised!"

"Are you kidding me?" Lilly's voice yelled from behind me. "Is Silvia your pimp or something?"

"Lilly!" I practically growled. "Don't say stuff like that." Hadn't she been taught manners?

Silvia laughed. At me. "You are *so* nice. I like you Zonta. You always have looked up to me." Then she glared at Lilly. "And if I were you, I would listen to Zonta. It is her house after all." Silvia walked over behind the couch and knocked the top of Owen's head. "Let's get out of here."

Owen, whose red-freckled face looked like it was on fire, jumped up and followed Silvia.

Chastity pulled down her very short skirt and ran her fingers through her hair, making sure the brown waves fell perfectly over her shoulders. Then she stuck her chin in the air and walked over to the stack of pizza boxes and grabbed four of them. "I'll take these to go. Got to have something to eat."

"Wait!" I moved quickly over to Silvia who was starting to head up the stairs. "I don't want *you* to leave. The party has just started."

Silvia sighed and watched Chastity walk past her, following Owen up the stairs. "Look, Zonta, I tried. I really did. But this really is *not* a party."

"ARE YOU COMING?" Chastity's voice echoed down the stairs. "OWEN IS REALLY PISSED."

Silvia rolled her eyes and yelled, "I'M COMING! TELL OWEN TO CALM DOWN!" My eyes grew wide and Silvia laughed at me again. "Zonta, close your mouth." I did, but my frown was still deep. "No,

Zonta, I am not a pimp." She shot a glare at Lilly who was still standing at the snack table staring at us. "I'm just a really good friend." She took one last look at the almost empty basement and added, "Something you are clearly *missing*." Then she was gone.

Chapter 7

Game

"Well, that went well!" Lilly's voice was the last thing I wanted to hear.

"Will you shut up!" I snapped.

Lilly's wild green eyes grew wide. "Wait a sec. Don't get pissy with me. I didn't throw a party without inviting friends."

I wanted to rip my mom's sweater off Lilly. But instead, I stood there, growling to myself. Suddenly, I heard a bunch of feet running down the stairs and turned to see who was making so much noise. I was shocked to see Vashon Wilkes and eight other guys stumbling into the basement. I didn't know the boys, but they were clearly freshmen. One had a gaming console under one arm, while two others carried some huge, plastic box. "Wow! What an awesome place you got here, Zonta!" Vashon's wide smile was pure joy. It snapped me out of my need to rip off Lilly's sweater.

"Thanks, Vashon." I smiled back. I didn't know him well, except that he helped Lilly and me call 911 to stop Ozzie from doing anything stupid. He was black, like Ozzie, and, like Ozzie, he was from Hall, Hancock's historically black neighborhood. I remembered how, only two weeks ago, Vashon and all of Hall united around Ozzie. Vashon's grandmother, Mrs. Wilkes, made food for Ozzie's family for a whole week. Or at least she made sure everyone in the neighborhood did their part. And, as Vashon and Ozzie explained, nobody messed with Mrs. Wilkes. In fact, it was Mrs. Wilkes whose words kept Ozzie from swallowing those pain pills. She made him believe he mattered.

I still couldn't understand why Ozzie thought he didn't matter. He had it all. He was a football star . . . no, *the* football star at Hancock High. He also had good grades, a caring family, people liked him, girls wanted him, and it seemed everyone wanted to be him. My stomach turned at the memory. I had shut Ozzie out when I broke up with him. I knew I had hurt him. I had been way more into him than he was into me. Still, he shouldn't have dated me because his friends had pushed him into it. It didn't matter how I tried to justify my actions. I hoped that I hadn't been one of Ozzie's reasons.

"Hope it's okay I invited Vashon and his friends?" Ozzie spoke softly, pulling me out of my thoughts. I hadn't noticed him walk up behind me, putting weight on his bad leg. I looked up at the towering football player who was still trying to prove he was my friend.

"No . . . I mean . . . yes . . . it's okay." I looked back at the sudden movement of furniture. Vashon's friends opened the huge plastic box and began to connect all sorts of gaming devices to our huge flat-screen. "Why are they here?"

Ozzie smiled. "Well, you said you invited a few *popular* people and hoped they would invite others. I realized, a little late, that I was one of those people." He shook his head at the thought. "So when no one showed up, I texted Vashon. He and his friends have been dying for a place to game all night." Ozzie glanced at all the food. "I thought you should have people over who would love to be here."

I smiled at Ozzie. I couldn't remember the last time I really smiled at him. Maybe we had both moved on. Or at least we were trying to. "Thanks, Ozzie." I looked at the gangly group of freshman boys who were already carrying the *whole* snack-food table closer to the couches. One little red-headed white boy glanced at me shyly and then looked away with flaming cheeks. Vashon laughed and teased the poor boy. It was the complete opposite of the scene that had played out on these very same couches only thirty minutes earlier.

"Good thing Silvia and her friends already left." Lilly came up to stand on the other side of me. "That would have been really weird."

Ozzie laughed. "But if Vashon and the rest of the gamers had arrived first, Chastity and Owen would have never set foot down here."

"Different kind of game," Lilly laughed.

"A better one," I sighed and pulled out my phone.

"Who are you calling?" Lilly asked.

"Hancock Pizza." I smiled. "I think we'll need a lot more food!"

Chapter 8

Tease

did u really send that pic?

Vonny texted. I finally had time to catch up with her the next morning. I plopped down on a basement couch next to an empty pizza box.

yes. tbh i think it was a bad idea. it might make him think im into him

idk. maybe hes just messing w/ u

i know hes messing w/ me and i want him to stop

i mean i think hes just teasing you. tbh it makes the most sense

I felt a little relief. If Carlos was just joking with me, then he'd leave me alone and move on to the next person to tease.

r u sure

it's the way guys r. think stupid jokes r funny. don't have a clue

I hoped she was right. But still, even if he was teasing, it messed with my head. I wouldn't completely chill out until I knew *for sure* that she was right.

Chapter 9

The Gift

As the days passed, I didn't hear from Carlos. So I stopped worrying so much. Maybe Vonny was right. Maybe it was all a stupid joke. Maybe he'd leave me alone when school started up again. At least that's what I hoped.

I also chilled out about Lilly. I mean, I tried not to think about how Lilly was taking over my house. After all, Christmas traditions seemed to always lift my spirit. Lilly didn't grow up with the same traditions. Or any, from what I saw. So it was sort-of fun to watch her be in awe of Mom's over-the-top decorations and the growing pile of gifts under the tree.

December 25th felt weird, though. Mom and Dad had enough gifts under the tree so Lilly had something to open, but still we had way more gifts. It felt like she was doing a lot of watching, so I wasn't as excited as usual. But I was happy that several of Lilly's gifts included new clothes and her own new black boots. They were combat-like and made of black leather. They had a practical sole, which would be better to use in bad weather. She also opened a box with one oversized, sky-blue sweater that she clearly liked because she pulled it on and didn't take it off.

"Great! Now you don't have to wear my clothes anymore!" I couldn't help myself.

"Zonta! That is not nice." Mom fussed at me.

"It's okay, Monta." Lilly said. "Trust me, I am ready to get out of those clothes. Too small, and not really my style!" Everyone laughed, except me. It felt weird every time Lilly called my parents by their first names. I thought for sure that Mom would make her to call them Mr. and Mrs. Jones. Those were the rules my parents taught me, but they weren't making Lilly follow the same rules. But I was trying to be nice, so I didn't point it out.

I enjoyed opening a small package that Vonny had sent me from California. It was a bracelet made of tiny white seashells. Right when I thought we were done opening gifts, Dad pulled out a small box with a huge red bow on it and handed it to Lilly. "Here. Monta and I talked, and we decided that we want you to have this."

"Thanks, Zeb," Lilly took the box and frowned just a little. "You're so serious. Do I need to worry?"

Mom laughed. "No, honey. We just want you to feel like you're part of the family."

My stomach dropped and my mouth might have opened in shock too. I tried to catch myself before Lilly saw me, but it was too late. She was already looking at me, so I threw on my best smile to try and cover my shock. She smiled back, but I could tell it was also forced.

"Okay, thanks," Lilly said, but my parents noticed the hesitation.

"Go on. Open it." Mom pointed at the box, hoping to break the sudden awkwardness. Lilly did open it. It was a phone. An expensive one. Confused, she looked up at my parents. So Mom explained, "This way you can reach us when you need to and we already have a tracking app on it. That way we always know where you are. You have no reason to be afraid." She squeezed Dad's hand before she added, "And we have no reason to be afraid for you."

I was surprised at Lilly's response. I expected her to be so excited and grateful, but she just stared. At the phone, then at my parents. When I saw the disappointment in my parents' eyes, I suddenly became angry. "Well, are you going to say something? Anything? Like *thank you, Mr. and Mrs. Jones*?"

"Zonta!" Mom fussed at me, again. "It's okay. I'm sure Lilly is just overwhelmed."

Lilly nodded quickly. "Yes, of course. Thank you!" She added a smile as she explained, "I've never gotten anything like this before."

"That's okay." Mom answered. "You can let it sink in." She and Dad were suddenly satisfied. They believed Lilly was honestly shocked by sheer joy and happiness.

But I wasn't fooled. Something was going on in her head and she wasn't telling us.

Chapter 10

Turkey

For hours, the smell of turkey spilled into every room in the house.

"It's like a different kind of torture." Lilly stood in the large opening between the kitchen and our living room. Mom and Dad were relaxing on the couch, each on their own phone. They were catching up on the latest news or gossip. I could never tell which one and didn't really care. I was taking it easy, spread out on the soft carpet near the tree, searching my own phone for the latest posts. I didn't even think about Carlos that day. Wrapping paper and gifts were still tossed all over the carpet, but no one moved to clean up the mess. Except, Lilly had quietly picked up her gifts and taken them to her room. We all guessed she was trying on her new clothes. We were right. She stood in front of us with her new jeans on, along with the same over-sized, blue sweater.

"What torture?" Mom asked Lilly as we all looked up from our phones.

Lilly moved to stand in front of us with the gas log fireplace behind her. The flames didn't give off much heat, but it made the room feel cozier. "Well, I'm used to being hungry. When I walk past a restaurant, the great smells make my hunger worse, so I quickly walk away. But here, the smell is everywhere. I can't escape it."

We all awkwardly laughed. We hadn't thought much about how hungry Lilly must have been some days. Mom, clearly happy that she was feeding Lilly, smiled. "You can get anything you want to eat while we wait for dinner to be ready."

"I know, but I still wanted to check. Thanks, Monta . . . I mean Mrs. Jones." Lilly glanced at me, making sure she had said it correctly.

My face warmed as my mother glared at me and then quickly turned to Lilly. "Lilly, it's okay. You can call me Monta." Lilly nodded and gave her a little smile and then walked back into the kitchen. I heard her open and close kitchen cabinets, but I didn't care. I did notice that she went straight to her room, instead of joining us. I was thankful for a little time alone with my parents, even if Mom gave me a lecture on how to make Lilly feel at home.

A couple of hours later, we all set the table for Christmas dinner. Lilly's eyes grew wider with every dish we placed like a huge puzzle onto the red tablecloth. As she put the mashed potatoes down, Mom yelled, "Make sure there is room for the rolls!"

Lilly looked at me and whispered, "Wow!" The spread was more than we could eat, but I knew it would also be dinner for the next three nights. Mom always insisted on eating leftovers, since wasting food was not a choice. Still, at that moment, it felt like too much.

I helped Lilly move over the green beans so she could put down the dish. "Trust me. It all looks great right now. But in a couple of days, you will be sick of leftovers." I hated feeling like I needed to excuse myself. It was my house after all. I was so tired of everyone thinking I was "rich," but I was afraid that this meal was one more proof against me. My parents always laughed when I told them that everyone thought I was rich. We *did* live in one of the nicer neighborhoods, but we *didn't* live on Lake Midway. Lake Drive was full of huge homes with fancy cars parked in front of their three-or-four-car garages. Half of Lake Drive was blocked off so the rest of Hancock could not use their private beaches. Instead, the rest of us had to use the public beach access. *Us.* I was one of those who had to *keep out* of the rich neighborhood. Yet, with the food staring up at me at that moment, I realized I was rich. At least, compared to Lilly.

"Not sure why you make it sound bad?" Lilly's voice broke into my thoughts. "I think it's great you'll have leftovers for days."

I realized Lilly wasn't calling me rich. It was all in my head. She was seriously impressed with the puzzle-layout of food. I smiled, for real.

"Listen! It's not just me eating these leftovers, you got to do your part too!"

"Okay, girls!" Dad walked up to the table with a bottle of wine. "Let's enjoy the meal first."

We all sat down, Dad said grace, and then we ate. And ate.

"Monta? Zeb?" Lilly's voice took our attention away from the music blaring from the other room.

"Yes, Lilly?" Mom and Dad said at the same time.

"I want to thank you for all you've done for me." Lilly had a serious look on her face. Before my parents could respond with kind words and blowing it off as no big deal, Lilly continued. "I need you to know that *I know* it has been a big sacrifice for you." She looked right at me as I lifted a roll to my mouth. "It's not easy having things change so fast." I put my roll back on my plate.

Mom jumped in. "Lilly, it's not—"

"But *it is*, Monta," Lilly interrupted and then smiled gently. "It is a huge deal, and I can never thank you enough for taking me in, housing me, clothing me, and feeding me." She looked at me. "Even if I was wearing clothes two sizes too small."

I laughed. "Well at least we have the same shoe size! I might borrow your new boots!"

Everyone laughed and we all returned to eating and talking about the snowstorm that was supposed to hit us early the next morning.

Something, though, had changed. It felt like Lilly was trying to tell us something. But we weren't listening.

Chapter 11

A Way Out

I woke up earlier than usual. There was just enough daylight that I could see the snow had started to come down. It looked thick and heavy. Soon the old dirty snow would have a fresh coat of white. But something in my stomach turned. Something was wrong.

I quickly threw an old sweatshirt over the t-shirt and shorts that I slept in almost every night. Mom had given up buying me new pj's a long time ago. My well-worn *I Love NYC* t-shirt was way too big when Dad bought it for me when we first visited New York City. I must have been ten, but I remember it like it was yesterday. It was the only place I had ever been where no one stared either at Mom for being black or Dad for being white as they held hands walking down the street. In New York, I didn't see those ever-changing looks. Those stares that came from people in most other places, some full of pity, others filled with curiosity. And then there were always those one or two offensive nods that screamed either *how dare you* OR *good for you*. But not in New York City. It was full of diversity. There was simply no other place in the world where so many races, religions, cultures, and languages lived together . . . each doing their own thing. At least, that's the way I saw it.

I had asked my parents why we couldn't live there, and they told me we could never afford to. I had begged them. But they said they wanted a big house, not a small condo. When I asked them how they could stand people looking at them all the time, they just smiled and said four things. "You get used to it. You deal with it. You decide it really doesn't matter. And, besides, it is more common than you think." I'd roll my eyes at them and then they'd fuss at me and tell me that I needed to stop thinking every place was better than Hancock. They would point out that I was liked by others, and it seemed, to them, that I didn't have *any* issues. So I needed to stop wishing my life away.

I pushed away my thoughts of NYC as I moved down the hallway toward the kitchen. The leftover cookies still sitting on the white granite countertops were the only sign that we hadn't quite cleaned up everything from last night. Mom and Dad were still asleep, and the house was quiet, so I pushed away that strange feeling. It had to be my head messing with me! I slipped into the living room to turn on the Christmas tree lights and the gas log fireplace. Never too early to make the house feel cozy. That was when I saw it. The box. Lilly's small gift box under the tree.

I frowned as I went to pick it up. I didn't notice it yesterday. I thought Lilly had taken it to her room. I picked it up, expecting a light, empty box. But it was not empty. I opened it and the phone was still inside. With a note. I unfolded the note.

Hi Zonta, Monta, and Zeb.

I know it sucks that I'm leaving the note. Sorry about that.

Time to go. Thanks for all you've done. Took my clothes (Not yours, Zonta ☺).

Hope it is okay I took some food and a few cans and a can-opener. Saw you had three of them. I took the oldest one. At least it looked the oldest. And I took some leftovers. Zonta, you won't have to eat as much of it the rest of the week ☺.

Don't worry about me. I got places I can hang. School starts back soon. I'll see you then, Zonta. Get on with your family thing.

Thanks again.

Lilly

My heart raced as I ran down the hall on the other side of the living room. It was the hallway to the guest room. No . . . to Lilly's room. The door was open. I ran inside and found the bed neatly made and all my old clothes neatly stacked.

Lilly was gone.

She had left. Not because she hated being here.

She left because of me.

I didn't have to be frustrated anymore. She gave me a way out.

I should have been excited or happy.

But I wasn't.

Chapter 12

Gone

Mom and Dad freaked out. The fresh snow had wiped away any chance of finding tracks. There was no sign anywhere of where Lilly might have gone. The police took all the info from Dad and told him they would look for her. Dad held his phone waiting to hear back from the police while Mom gripped Lilly's phone for over an hour. She couldn't believe Lilly didn't take it with her.

"At least she took my jacket," Mom said as she stood in front of the window looking out at the blanket of white.

"And the red wool cap I bought her." Dad came up behind Mom and squeezed her empty hand. He then peeled the phone out of her other hand. "I'm sure she's okay."

Mom watched Dad shove Lilly's phone in his jeans back pocket, while he still held his own phone in his hands. "How did she carry everything? She didn't take any of our suitcases and her old camo backpack wasn't big enough for all the food she took *and* her clothes."

"I'll ask her when I see her at school," I said out loud. Mom and Dad both looked at me. Shocked. "What?" I asked confused by their reaction.

"Zonta. Aren't you upset?" Mom was looking me up and down as if she could find a clue from what I was wearing. "Why haven't you called any of your friends to ask if they know where she is?" I realized she was not looking at my shorts and sweatshirt, she was looking for my phone. It wasn't on me.

"Oh. Good idea." I quickly turned my back on my parents and ran down the hall to my room. I grabbed the phone off my bed where I had fallen asleep with it the night before. When I looked at my screen, I wondered who I should call? Or text? Who would answer me so early in the morning? Who even cared? Only two names came to mind. Ozzie and Vashon. I messaged them both.

have u seen lilly?

No answer. I told my parents I would let them know when I heard from someone. Everyone was still asleep. I didn't tell them that I only texted two people. I didn't know anyone else who knew Lilly. I didn't really have any other friends who cared. Silvia and Chastity sure wouldn't care. And I didn't text Vonny. How could she help anyway? She had never even met Lilly.

I sat on my bed for the next four hours and stared at my screen.

nope. whats up

Ozzie's text made me jump. I quickly responded.

shes gone. left. omg mom and dad freaking out

I stared at the screen waiting for Ozzie's text. I hoped he had answers.

u sure?

yes took her stuff

k. she cant b far

said she has places to hang. u know what she means?

nope. sorry

dont know what 2 do

tbh i don't have a clue

Ozzie had only recently become friends with Lilly. I believed him. He was probably worried too. More than me, actually. I didn't know what else to say. I finally texted.

k. will let u know if i find her

k. thnx

I waited a second to get up and walk to tell my parents that Ozzie didn't have a clue. Suddenly, I felt my phone vibrate. I wondered what else Ozzie had to say. But it wasn't Ozzie. It was Vashon. I had forgotten that I had included both of them in the text.

sure lilly will b fine. just chill

Ozzie responded before I could.

she with u?

Vashon quickly texted.

she came by then left. said 2 tell u she will b fine. so i did

I quickly asked.

u know where she went?

no. but the big black plastic bag she was carrying was full of stuff. she cant b far

Ozzie asked.

did u follow her?

no

why not

2 cold

I could tell Ozzie was pissed.

u r stupid. u let lilly take off in the snow?

When Vashon didn't respond, I did.

Vashon? u there?

He still didn't respond. Ozzie added.

u really going 2 leave us on read?

Two minutes later Vashon finally texted.

lilly is gone. she wants to be gone. not much we can do when she wants to be gone. so chill. K?

Chapter 13

Dumped On

"Why would she do this?" Mom cried. "I thought she liked it here. Liked us."

My stomach hurt. Had I really chased her away? Had I hurt her feelings and made her feel unwelcome? My parents went on and on *and* on about Lilly and it was just too much. So I finally I shared my thoughts on why I believed Lilly left.

"Are you serious?" Mom's voice was almost scary. "You thought Lilly wouldn't live with us very long?"

"Well . . . yes," I whispered. The wide-eyed look on my parents' faces told me that Lilly's words *get on with your family thing* suddenly made sense to them. I was to blame for Lilly leaving.

"Why in the hell would you think that?" Dad yelled. He was not quiet and scary like Mom. He was outright angry. "You think a girl gets beat up and then, like some fairy tale, everything is good again?" Dad looked at Mom. "Monta, I thought we raised a kind and sweet young lady. Don't know what happened to her because she's been replaced by a selfish child."

I felt tears well up. Dad had never called me a selfish child before. How could I make them understand? "Well, she *looked* and *acted* all good again!" I wiped my eyes with the back of my hand.

Mom took a deep breath. "Zonta, of course she looked and acted okay. She felt safe." Mom walked over to the window. The snow was so deep now that you couldn't see where the road stopped and the sidewalks started. A few neighbors were bundled up and trying to get ahead of the pile of snow. The only thing keeping Dad from already clearing our drive was me.

"And now she is somewhere out in this mess!" Mom kept staring at the falling snow.

"But Vashon said she was okay, Mom." I offered. "And I believe him."

"And this is a boy you hardly know. Right?" Dad jumped in. When I nodded, he shook his head, clearly baffled by me. "And why would you believe him?"

It took me a minute. My parents were upset. Really upset. And they thought I didn't know what I was talking about at all. They never did really understand how I saw things. They had always asked me to explain myself to help them follow my thought process. I never felt like I could explain because I never understood why they were confused. There were so many times when *they* said things and I didn't get what *they* were saying. I'd catch parts of it. But then when I put those parts together, they would tell me that that was *not* what they had said.

When I was in third grade, they put me on ADHD meds. It helped. A lot. I could finally listen to the teachers without being so distracted by everyone else in the class or by the thoughts in my head, which always took me down a more interesting path. I could control what I needed to focus on. At least for the most part. And my grades improved.

But the problem was that Mom and Dad thought taking the meds meant I was fixed. I was not *fixed*. I still thought very differently than they did. It didn't take long for them to figure that out. So they slowly accepted that I was wired differently and that it was *not* about *fixing* me. Mostly, though, they *were* patient. Especially when it came to schoolwork. But at that very moment, they were not patient. They were pissed. They were pissed at my thinking. They were pissed that I had been unkind to Lilly. They were pissed at me.

"Zonta!" Mom interrupted my thoughts. "Answer your father! Why do you believe Vashon?"

I looked at both my parents, holding back any more tears from falling. As awful as I felt, I *did* know what I was talking about! It was simple. "Because Vashon is the only person in all of Hancock that ever gave a damn about Lilly *before* she was beat up."

Silence.

I was right. My parents and I, even Ozzie, only cared about Lilly once something had happened to her. Not before.

Chapter 14

Found

The police called Dad the next day. They told him that they found Lilly. She had given them permission to tell us that she was back with her aunt on the corner of 19th Street and Maple. As the officer spoke, Dad wrote down Lilly's address and nodded eagerly. He was ready to go pick her up. But, when Dad told the officer that he'd go get her as soon as the roads were clear, the officer said no.

Lilly didn't want to come back. Said that her aunt's boyfriend was gone.

The police couldn't make Lilly come with them.

We had to move on.

Still, Dad slowly pinned Lilly's address on the small bulletin board in the kitchen. He would be ready if she changed her mind.

I wanted to feel relieved. I wanted to yell, "See, I told you!" But didn't. Even though I had my family back, something had changed.

Chapter 15

New Year's Eve

I didn't go to a New Year's Eve party. And I didn't even think about throwing a party. We were all invited across the street to the Hembys' house, which had become a New Year's Eve tradition. My parents did not push me when I said I didn't want to go. I didn't feel like explaining that I didn't want to be around Silvia, or any of her friends that might turn up. And even though I hadn't thought about Carlos in over a week, I didn't want to risk that it might be *the* party Silvia threw that he would want to go to.

Instead, I told my parents that I needed to study. And, by studying all day, I showed them I wasn't coming up with a lame excuse. Mom and Dad didn't argue since they were pushing me to take the SAT as many times as I could, which meant I had to take the first one in March. I could take it again in the fall. Mom made it sound like I should take it two or three more times.

"Why would I want to take it again?" I asked Mom as I sat at the dining room table with my study guide spread out in front of me.

Yellow, blue and green sticky-notes not only marked pages but were also stuck all over the table in front of me.

"Whatever it takes to get scores good enough to get into a good college." Mom answered as she folded dish towels. She had a few minutes before she needed to get ready for the party.

"But what if my score is good the first time that I take it?" I asked. I was confused with her reasoning.

Mom didn't answer right away. She was trying to figure out the best way to respond. "Zonta, just keep your options open."

"Really, Mom?" I was not happy. "You really don't think I have a chance at doing well. You think I'm stupid."

"I did *not* say that!" Mom put down the dish towel, and one hand rested on her hip. "I believe you will do great. I only want you to leave your options open and not settle for a low score."

"Okay, so you *are* saying that I will get a low score." My mouth dropped. "That's the same thing as saying I'm stupid and won't do well the first time. Thanks, Mom!" I stood up and started to close my notebook.

"What're you doing?" Mom was confused.

"Well, if I won't do well anyway, then why study?" I pushed down the tears that began to well up. I hated being angry and crying at the same time.

"That is *not* what I am saying!" Mom left her pile of half-folded dish towels and walked over to me. She put her hand on my shoulder. "Look at me, Zonta." I did, but I was glaring at her. However, I did let her hold on to my shoulder. "I do think you can do well. I do NOT think you are stupid. But I do know it takes longer for you to learn things sometimes. But when you know it, you know it." I softened my glare, but only a little. "I am only thinking that maybe the first time through you will get a good idea of what comes easy and what is hard. Then you will know what you need to focus on re-learning. That's all I meant."

I took a deep breath. She wasn't wrong. But still, it didn't make complete sense. "It seems that I should figure all that out *before* I take the first test. Isn't that why I'm studying now?"

Mom looked down at my notebook and all my sticky notes I had placed on the table. I was clearly trying. Suddenly, a huge smile appeared. "You are right, Zonta! I know exactly what will help."

My eyebrows rose. "What?"

"We need to make sure you have everything you need to do your best the first time through." She grabbed both of my shoulders and looked right into my eyes. Like she was getting ready to share some big news. "We will get you a tutor."

I was not sure what I expected her to say. Maybe that she and Dad would help me study. But a tutor? I didn't want some stranger judging me. I didn't need to have someone else try to figure me out. I didn't have time for that. "Who?" I asked.

"Not sure. But someone perfect!" She turned to head down the hall toward her bedroom. I heard her yell, "Don't worry, I know exactly who to talk to. I'll ask Cindy tonight at the party. She knows everybody."

Great. All I needed was Mrs. Hemby, Silvia's mom, in my business. But maybe she wouldn't tell Silvia. Maybe. I looked outside the window and watched as the last hint of the sun disappeared. The Hembys' living room lights began to draw attention to what was happening inside their elegant home. Clearly, they were preparing for the party. They would celebrate the New Year without me. What Mom and Dad didn't know was that I planned to stop studying as soon as the party started. I'd thaw some pizza and watch old 80's movies. Maybe I'd text Vonny and maybe not. I was looking forward to doing what I wanted to do.

But all of a sudden, I felt guilty. I tried not to think of Lilly, but I couldn't help it. I hoped she was safe. I never looked forward to going back to school before, but Tuesday couldn't come fast enough. I couldn't wait to step foot back in Hancock High because I'd know for sure how Lilly was *really* doing.

Chapter 16
Tuesday

Hancock High's halls were busy with everyone talking and laughing. I pulled out some books from my locker and I tried to not look obvious as I scanned the halls for Lilly. I hoped that I would be able to talk to her before class started.

"Did you talk to her yet?" Ozzie came up next to me with his book bag slung over a shoulder with his Browns cap tucked into the side of it. He was walking like he used to, except he still wore the fancy brace that gave him some protection.

"Not yet." I smiled and pointed at his knee. "Looks like you're doing better." It felt good talking to Ozzie like we were old friends. It had been fun at my party once Vashon and his friends showed up. Thanks to Ozzie!

Ozzie leaned against the locker next to mine. "Well, good enough for surgery on my ACL tomorrow. Then I start all over again. I should be in physical therapy for a while."

"So this means you might be able to play football next fall?" I smiled. I was happy for him. He was a huge football star at Hancock High and had missed out on playing in the championship game. It seemed to me that even though the Hancock Thunder had taken home the State Championship, their star player was not happy he missed out. After all, he helped the team pull off a winning season. At least that was what I was told. I wasn't too great at keeping up with all the details, but it made sense.

Ozzie pushed himself off the locker and shifted his book bag to his other shoulder. "We'll see." He smiled, but it was forced. He looked over my shoulder and added, "I think we better get to class."

He didn't want to talk about football. Seemed crazy to me since it was his life. But I didn't push him on it, so I nodded, and we both headed to first period a little early.

First period U.S. History was the only class that didn't change for our second semester. It was a relief knowing that Lilly was in my first period class. I didn't have to hunt down the whole school to talk to her. I dreaded seeing Carlos. But I knew what to expect in U.S. History and from my teacher, Ms. Williams. So I told myself I'd be okay.

"Hi there, sweet momma." Carlos's creepy voice made me rethink how I felt about first period. I knew he was talking to me, but I ignored him and went straight to my old seat. I hoped Carlos wouldn't bring up how he texted me before Christmas. I wanted to pretend it had never happened.

"Shut up, Carlos!" Ozzie said as he sat at the table and chair that he claimed as his desk. I felt relief but didn't look over at Ozzie. I didn't want to give Carlos any attention. But when I heard someone move, I glanced over to see what was going on.

Carlos walked up to Ozzie, plopped his butt on the desk, and looked down at Ozzie. It was hard to look down at Ozzie. Even sitting, he was huge, but Carlos was also tall. "You still hot for the girl?" Carlos asked, as if I wasn't even in the room. I looked around and only Blake Dockins and Mateo Meza-Moya were at their desks. I made a mental note not to come early to class again. Blake, Carlos's blond creeper-sidekick, was watching the scene. Mateo was a heavy-set Hispanic boy that I rarely talked to. He didn't even look up from his phone. He was wearing his white earbuds and acted like the rest of us didn't exist. He'd pull them out when the teacher arrived, but not before. I didn't really know Mateo, even though he and I did have to work on a project together last semester. But we divided up our sections and worked on each part on our own. I quickly learned that Mateo didn't want to say or do more than he had to.

Ozzie looked at Carlos and sucked air through his teeth. "Not a chance! You know, I thought you were calling *me* sweet momma. And I just don't feel that way about you, Carlos." There was a second of silence before Carlos and Blake broke into laughter. Even Mateo's eyes shifted for a second, before he looked away. Ozzie laughed and shoved Carlos off his desk. "Now get off my desk and find someone else to flirt with."

Other students walked through the door as Carlos punched Ozzie's shoulder. Ozzie punched him back. Blake was still laughing as Carlos headed to sit in his own desk next to his friend. Within minutes, the room was full. I ignored Chastity Shaw as she walked in and flung herself into a seat in the middle of the room. But I couldn't unsee the memory of Owen Hemby and her on my couch. I was thankful when Ms. Williams walked in, since I needed to focus on something else. Not Chastity, and for sure not Carlos! As our teacher took off her jacket and placed it on the back of her chair, I finally made eye contact with Ozzie. Even though he couldn't hear me, I whispered, "Thank you." His face was suddenly serious, and he barely nodded as he turned to face our teacher.

Something had changed in Ozzie. Or maybe in me. I had stopped thinking of him as my ex-boyfriend. And I had begun to think of him as someone I should just be nice to after all he had been through. Even though I didn't understand what was going on in his head, he was trying to make up for being such a jerk. He'd proven that at the party. But, at that moment, I realized he was looking out for me. Not because he wanted me. But because we were friends. I was thankful.

Chapter 17

Catch

Lilly was late. Of course. When she lived with me, we were always on time. But now that she was back with her aunt, she was late. She gave me a quick wave when she came in, which made me smile. Once first period was over, I thought I could grab her, but she was one of the first to slip out the door. She wasn't avoiding me, was she? I hoped not. I made a new plan and decided to talk to her at lunch. I thought maybe that would be best anyway since we might actually get a few minutes to talk.

My mind was on Lilly, so it took me a minute to gather all my things. Suddenly Carlos stood next to me. "Why don't you send me a different pic?" He asked as he undressed me with his eyes. I froze, but my eyes scanned the room. The teacher was at her desk talking to the only other kid left. "I'd really like a pic of . . ." Carlos's eyes dropped to my chest.

My heart raced and my hand began to shake as I looked away. I closed up my laptop and stacked my notebook on top. I had to think.

No big deal. This was no big deal, since he was just a stupid guy doing stupid things! I looked up at him and forced a smile. "You're funny!"

He stepped in closer and let his eyes rest on my lips. "I'm not trying to be funny, baby." Then he licked his lips. I wanted to puke.

I swallowed. Be nice. I had to be nice, since he didn't know better. I dropped my smile and put on my best look of concern. "I'm sorry, Carlos. I'm sure you're a nice guy, but I'm really *not* into you. So please don't ask me again." There! I had told him. I let him down easy.

But Carlos didn't look upset. He leaned in even closer, and I could feel his breath on my ear. "Don't worry. You'll come around and see I'm quite a catch."

The stink of his breath only fed my need to gag. Hadn't he heard what I had said? Suddenly the next class started walking through the door. I was relieved. I decided the best thing was to stop talking and just leave. As I began to lift my pile of things up to my chest, Carlos reached out and grabbed my left hand. Hard. I turned and faced him. Shocked. It hurt. Then he loosened his grip, but he didn't let go. He started to rub it. Gently. When I tried to pull away, he'd grip it again. "Please, let go," I said as calmly as I could. He was creeping me out!

"Your hand is so soft, like I thought it would be. After looking at it every night for the last few weeks I feel like it's already mine to hold."

He licked his lips again and it looked like he was going to bend down and kiss it.

I jerked my hand away as hard as I could. Finally free from his grip. "I need you to stop it." I said firmly. "I'm never going to be with you. So delete that stupid pic and move on." I took a deep breath, grabbed my pile of stuff, and turned to leave.

"We'll see about that." Carlos whispered. I didn't turn around. I was done. I hoped that he could see that I meant it. My stomach burned. What if he was doing more than teasing me? What if he would never leave me alone? I pushed the thought away. He was just a stupid guy. That was all. Just stupid.

Chapter 18

Lunch

I was thankful I didn't have any more classes with Carlos. And I hoped I'd be okay at lunch, since I was going to find Lilly and sit with her. As expected, Lilly was with Vashon and his group of friends. I knew there was no way Carlos would want to sit with a bunch of freshman boys. Feeling some relief, I took my lunch tray and headed to their table.

"Is it okay if I sit here?" I noticed Lilly glare at me briefly and then look back at her fries, but I stuck to my plan. I didn't bother looking around for an empty table, mostly because I didn't want to see if Carlos was looking for me. Sitting with Lilly and Vashon had to work!

The talking stopped and Vashon smiled up at me. "Sure, Zonta." He pointed at a seat. "I think Colin would love you to sit next to him." The little red-headed, white boy, from my party, suddenly had red cheeks, again. But he didn't say anything and scooted his tray a little away from me, making sure I had enough room. His shyness was such a breath of fresh air compared to Carlos. But the best part was that it was the perfect seat because it was across from Lilly.

"Hi, Lilly," I said, ignoring the teasing comments the other boys were throwing at poor Colin.

"Hi, Zonta." Lilly's wild green eyes softened as she smiled and bit into one of her fries. "Mmmmm. These are so good. You've got to try them."

I reached down and grabbed one off my tray. I guess I expected something amazing, but it still tasted greasy and bland to me. "They're the same as always." Lilly grinned, satisfied with my disappointment. "Very funny!" I threw a french fry at her, happy she was messing with me. As I smiled, I leaned in to ask, "Are you okay?"

Lilly's eyes darted over to the boys who were already lost in arguing about who really won their last video-game night. Colin may have wanted to sit next to me, but he sure wasn't interested in what we were talking about. None of the boys were. Lilly finally answered me. "Sure. Of course. All good. I'm great."

"Okay, that means *no*." I looked at her. She was trying to avoid eye contact.

"I just told you I was fine." She looked at her fries. Not me.

"No, you just told me four different ways that you are fine, which is overkill and clearly means you are *not* fine." I didn't touch my food as I continued to look at her. I tried to show her that I was ready to listen to her. I wanted her to see that I cared.

She finally looked at me. Paused. Then started laughing. "You really are crazy, you know?"

I frowned. "What is that supposed to mean?"

Lilly took another bite, swallowed, and then answered, "Why do you suddenly care about if I'm okay? You didn't care to come find me."

"That's not true! Dad called . . ." I wasn't too sure how to go on. I looked down at my fries and picked one up.

"Dad! That's right. Your dad called." Lilly was trying not to get angry. "It was Zeb and Monta . . . no, *excuse me* . . . Mr. and Mrs. Jones who were trying to reach out to me."

My stomach turned. Did she have to point out how rude I had been about her calling my parents by their first names? I had to prove that she was wrong about me. I did care! "Wait a second." I held up my fry and pointed it at her. "I texted Ozzie and Vashon and Vashon told me that you said not to worry." I suddenly pointed the fry at Vashon. "*He* told me not to worry." Couldn't she see that I had only done what I thought she wanted me to do?

"Hey. You all talking about me?" Vashon jumped in. A huge smile flashed across his face. "You know, I'm sitting right here."

Lilly touched Vashon's arm and smiled. "Don't worry about it."

Vashon shrugged his shoulders. "Alright! Whatever." He turned his head and jumped right back into the heated discussion on the other side of him.

I was quiet. I popped the french fry into my mouth, but it was hard to swallow. Lilly finally broke the silence between us. "You're right. Vashon told you not to worry. So you didn't. I don't get you, Zonta. You come across as a nice girl who cares about others, but it doesn't run very deep." I didn't have the words to explain it from my point of view. The more I said, the worse I made it. I felt my eyes begin to burn. I tried really hard not to cry. I couldn't let her see me cry.

I quickly stood up. "Got to go." The boys barely noticed, except Colin, who gave me an awkward wave and then quickly looked away.

"Zonta." Lilly could see I was on the edge of losing it. "Listen, if it makes you feel any better, I'm used to it. So don't worry about me."

I frowned. What did that even mean? My stomach twisted and I felt like puking. There was no way I was staying in the lunchroom. I didn't want Lilly to see how upset I was, but I also didn't want Carlos to talk to me. I quickly rushed to the huge trash cans and tossed out the rest of my fries. I shoved my plastic food tray onto the tall, metal rack that was already holding returned lunch trays.

I couldn't get out of there fast enough. I hoped no one would try to talk to me as I made my escape. I wasn't that lucky.

Chapter 19

The Note

"Here!" A hand shot in front of my face. It was holding a neatly folded note.

I followed the arm to find Emma Tang-Lee staring at me. Almost bored. She clearly did not care that I was on the verge of tears. Or that we were standing next to the dirty lunch trays. I knew Emma. She was in U.S. History with me and we had been in several classes together over the years. Even talked, when we had to, in class. About assignments. I knew her, but we never talked outside of class.

She finally looked at my face, where some tears had escaped. She dropped her arm with the note in it and sighed. "Boy problems?"

"No!" I frowned.

"Okay, good." She didn't really want to know. "Here!" She lifted the note back up to my face.

"What is it?" I didn't take it.

Emma's eyebrows lifted in disbelief. "Really? It's a note." She held it up, unfolded it and folded it again. "See?" I was a little surprised at how she was talking to me like I was an idiot. "Here!"

"I know it's a note. I'm not stupid." I began to reach for it before I stopped. "But who is it from?" I didn't know who to trust? What if it was from Carlos? It would be just like him to use Emma to give me a nasty note from him.

"You're killing me!" Emma rolled her eyes. She grabbed my hand and placed the note in it. "Take it."

I looked down at the note. In the most perfect handwriting, it said *Ms. Zonta Jones*. I stared at it. Confused. It was definitely *not* from Carlos. Who would be so formal and yet fold the paper into a tiny note? I looked at Emma who was staring at me like I was strange. "Why are you giving me this note?"

Emma rolled her eyes again. She moved in closer. "Listen. It was not my idea. But my brother asked me to give you a letter. Well, that was *not* happening. I was in no way hauling a huge letter around. So he wrote it like this." When I didn't say anything, she shook her head. "Open it! It's something about tutoring you. Which you *evidently* need . . . I don't *really* know. I only skimmed the letter. Not that I really care. Except . . ." She gave me a glare. "Don't you think for a minute he will be into you. He's not into girls like you."

And with a quick spin away from me, Emma was gone. I felt like I had been slapped. *Girls like me?*

I quickly shook off Emma's harsh judgement of me. Clearly the false rumor, from a few months ago about Ozzie and me, had spread through the whole school. But the truth had not. I walked away from the trash cans and went down the hall into the bathroom. I locked myself in a stall and opened the letter.

Dear Ms. Zonta Jones,

My name is Joseph Tang-Lee and your mother contacted me to tutor you in preparation for the SAT. I apologize for not emailing you, but I did not want to seem forward in my approach. I thought if my sister gave you this note, then you could trust that I am legit.

Please call me.

Sincerely,

Joseph Tang-Lee

I suddenly started laughing. Hard. This guy really thought this was the best way to approach me. Legit was one thing. But strange? Yes, this was strange. I looked at the number at the bottom of the page and pulled out my phone.

At least this would be a good distraction.

Chapter 20

Joseph

There were still a few minutes left before lunch was over, so I decided to text Joseph. No way was I going to actually call him.

hi got your note about tutoring

I looked at my screen for about two minutes, before I caught myself. What was I doing? I didn't know this guy and suddenly I was staring at the screen, waiting for my tutor to respond. My phone vibrated.

Zonta?

yes

How many people did he send notes to about tutoring? Of course it was me!

Nice to meet you. When is a good time to meet and begin tutoring? And where would you like to meet?

idk

I questioned why I was so quick to contact him. Was I really so desperate to get my mind off Carlos and Lilly? I looked at the note again. What if Joseph was a nice guy? But what if he was as rude as his sister? What if he only wanted to tutor me for the money. I growled at myself. Of course he was doing it for the money. He didn't know me and from Emma's reaction, what he did know was probably pretty bad.

I looked back at my phone feeling stupid. I really didn't know where or when we should meet. I hadn't thought about it at all. I should have waited and talked to Mom first so she could tell me more about this guy.

It took a few moments before he responded.

Will 17th Street Café work on Tuesdays and Thursdays after school?

As much as I was thankful that Joseph came up with a time and place, I frowned. There was no way I was being tutored down the street from Hancock High, especially across the street from Starbucks. Everyone would see us. I didn't want people to know I had a tutor.

The bell rang ending lunch period. I had to get to my next class. I had an idea.

tues and thurs are good. can u meet at bence's good vibes @ 3:30

Bence's Good Vibes was far away from Hancock High and near my house in the southern part of town. Mostly, older people met there. They liked the retro-70's feel, and the lounge area in the corner that reminded them of back-in-the-day with colorful couches and huge bean-bags. The owners thought it would also bring in my generation. But it was hard to compete with the Delgado Outdoor Mall on the northern side of town and all the coffee shops and pizza places near the high school.

I left the bathroom stall and quickly headed down the hall to my next class, Principles of Business & Finance. It was my first day in this class, so I sat down at the empty desk near the windows. At that moment, my phone vibrated. I looked down one last time.

Yes, that will work. I will see you on Thursday.

Suddenly, I dreaded Thursday.

Chapter 21

3rd Period

As class started, I glanced around the room to see if I knew anyone. I was surprised to find Emma Tang-Lee and Blake Dockins in the class. They clearly chose seats as far from each other as they could. I guessed that Emma had not recovered from Blake's racist remarks a few months ago in U.S. History. I didn't blame her. But at that moment I was still getting over her basically calling me trashy. So I didn't make eye contact with her and kept looking around the room.

There were a few other faces I recognized and some I had never seen before. I was thankful that Carlos was not in the class with Blake. Blake seemed to be less of a creep when he was alone. But I still didn't trust him.

As I continued to check out the room, I twisted in my seat to look directly at the seat behind me. A white girl with brown hair, that had clearly been straightened, looked back at me. Two drastically different earrings hung from each ear. One looked like a twisted silver corkscrew, the other a golden hoop. She looked sort of tall, but I couldn't quite tell with her sitting. "What?" Her brown eyes narrowed.

"Oh, nothing." I said and quickly turned to face the front. The teacher was taking his sweet time writing something on the board as the class was busy talking. I didn't recognize the girl. Was she new or was she someone I just didn't know? Wait. What if she was new like Lilly was new at the beginning of the year? It would be hard to move schools in the middle of the year. She might need a new friend. Or what if it was someone that I had grown up with and just didn't recognize? That would be embarrassing. But what if she *was* new? Like Lilly?

I swung back around to face the girl. I had to ask. "Hi, I'm sorry. I just was looking to see if I knew anybody in the class. I'm Zonta Jones. Are you new here?"

The girl looked around the room at everyone talking and then back at me. "Yeah. I'm new. I'm Mary Ann Daniels." She nodded politely.

I smiled broadly. "Welcome to Hancock High."

Mary Ann smiled awkwardly. In fact, she was almost laughing. "Are you the welcoming committee or something?"

I lost my smile and turned back to face the front. I was too eager. I stared at the back of the teacher, who was still writing. Why couldn't he start the class already! Suddenly, I felt a tapping on my shoulder. I turned back to face Mary Ann again. I felt stupid.

"Listen, Zonta." She smiled for real this time. "Thanks for welcoming me." I nodded but didn't know what to say. So she continued, "I'm . . . well . . . you see . . . not used to anyone welcoming me."

"What? That doesn't make sense." I frowned, trying to cover up my desire to grin since I was excited that she was actually talking to me.

Mary Ann smiled and explained, "Sure it does. When you move from school to school you get used to everyone already having their own lives. And why should they care about someone new? Hey, I'll probably be out of here by the end of the year anyway."

I let my smile loose and grinned. "Well. I care." I said it. It sounded so cliché. But I meant it. She needed me. Mary Ann needed me.

I'd prove to Lilly that my kindness did run deep. If there was one thing I did know, it was how to be kind to others. Kind *and* nice. As soon as I thought it, something turned in my stomach. But I didn't listen to it. Instead, I listened to the teacher finally call the class to attention.

Chapter 22
Thursday

"What's wrong?" Mary Ann asked as she took a bite of her apple. We had eaten lunch together Tuesday and Wednesday. She was okay. *Okay* seemed vague, but that was all I felt about her at that moment. We had no history, so we had nothing to remember and laugh about. Not like with Vonny, where every little thing reminded us *of a time*. I missed Vonny, but I was trying to be friends with Mary Ann. She needed me and I needed to prove I was still a kind person. I tried to pay attention to her talking about the last high school she was in and what had happened there, but I really didn't care. Who were these people she was talking about? But I didn't ask her because I was afraid that she might actually tell me. I had clearly let my mind wander and she saw it. I wasn't sure what to say, so I did the right thing and settled on the truth.

"I'm worried about this afternoon. I'm meeting a tutor for the first time. He's supposed to help me with my SAT prep." I half smiled. There it was. Nothing about what she had been talking about. Maybe she wouldn't be upset.

"So is it some creepy, old guy?" She teased and then pointed at the front of the black hoodie she was wearing. A scary pale face that looked like it was screaming, was staring at me. "Mr. Munch and I understand!"

I laughed. I guessed she was referring to the artist of the screaming, scary pale face but I wasn't sure. It didn't matter. I was thankful she wasn't upset with me for *not* paying attention. "No. It's a guy who graduated last year. He's really smart."

Mary Ann took another bite of apple. "So what are you worried about?"

I frowned. "Not really sure." I couldn't explain how the neatly folded letter and perfect-sentence texts seemed a little weird. "I guess I'm afraid he won't be good tutoring me because he is really, really smart."

"So?" Mary Ann said, once again. "You can just fire him and hire a dumb tutor." She grinned with a little juice from her apple dripping from the side of her mouth. "Because, you see, *everyone knows* dumb tutors are the best tutors! Really get your money's worth!"

I looked at her and smirked. "Very funny!"

Mary Ann wiped her mouth on her napkin. "Look. You should be happy you can even have a tutor to help you. Most can't even afford it." My stomach dropped. Was she really going to point out that I was a poor-little-rich-girl? That I should count my blessings because no one else had what I had?

"Okay," I responded. My cheeks began to warm. How dare she make me feel guilty! I didn't want to say anything rude. But I was afraid that if I stayed, I would say something I would regret.

Just as I was ready to make some lame excuse to leave the table, she put down her apple core on her tray and added, "My dad has paid for tutors at every high school I've ever been in." She laughed. "It seems hauling your only daughter around from city to city as a single dad made him feel pretty guilty." When I didn't say anything, she continued. "I enjoyed my tutors. Some were old, some were young. In any case, it was sometimes the only people I could count on talking to me. Even if they were paid."

"Were you called rich too?" I asked before I realized I had said it out loud.

"What? We were talking about tutors." She was clearly confused.

"Sorry . . . never mind." I quickly began to busy myself with putting my napkin on my tray. I hoped that it looked like I had not paid attention again. It would look like I was a total air-head, but that was better than fussing about being called a rich kid.

"Wait a minute." Mary Ann had an ah-ha look on her face. "People here give you flack for being rich?"

My cheeks grew warm again, but not from anger. I was so embarrassed! Had I really just told the new girl one of the things that bothered me? A thing my parents told me was too silly to deal with. "Well, not exactly. It's stupid, really. They just think I'm rich when I'm not."

"Well, of course you're not!" She smiled again.

"What?" I was confused. That wasn't the answer I expected. She had my full attention.

Mary Ann leaned in like she had a secret. "Well, if you *were* rich, you'd be in some private school or shipped away to some fancy boarding school." One finger pointed in the air, like an idea had just magically popped into her head. "Or, most obviously, this would NOT be your first tutor."

I felt something shift. I was free to talk about this *silly thing*. "So why does everyone think I'm rich?"

Mary Ann leaned back in her chair. Looked me over. "I'm pretty sure not *everyone* thinks you're rich. I don't."

I sat back in my chair and stared at this new girl. Her brown hair was pulled back in two short pony-tails. She stared back at me with those intense brown eyes. "So you're rich. Right?"

Mary Ann's eyes grew big and she laughed so loud that I didn't dare look to see if anyone was staring at us. "According to you or according to the janitor? *Or*, according to the couple that just bought their third yacht?"

I frowned. "Seems like it depends."

"Right." Mary Ann smiled, and her voice softened. "Look, Zonta. I know you've lived here your whole life, but no matter where you go, people will judge you for *something*. So you got two choices." I wasn't sure I wanted to hear her two choices, but I clearly couldn't stop her. "You either let others paint your portrait that defines who you are, or you paint your own picture. Some people will get to see who you really are, but some people never will. And *then* you stop focusing on those who see only what they want to see."

"But that is easier said than done." I argued. Quietly.

"Is it?" she whispered back.

I stared at Mary Ann for a moment. In awe. "You've figured it out. Haven't you?"

She laughed again. But not as loud. "Not all the way. But I'm working on it. Doesn't help much moving all the time. But it lets me reinvent who I want to be. Like a clean slate." She looked at me. It looked almost like pity. "That's what will make it harder for you. You can't just get a do-over." Then sadness filled her, and I saw her push down whatever was beginning to come to the surface. "But trust me, do-overs aren't great either. Can't have those friends where we can talk forever about things that *remind-us-of-a-time*."

My heart sunk. I felt so sorry for her. But then I felt something I hadn't felt in a while. Connected. Mary Ann *did* need me. But it looked like I needed her more.

Chapter 23

Tutor

With my black winter jacket already halfway off one shoulder, I stood at the door and scanned the restaurant, looking for Joseph. Bence's Good Vibes was just as I remembered it. A whole wall was covered with vinyl records and the floor was still covered in linoleum. The lime-green, plastic-looking floor was supposed to be an exact copy of the 70's. I looked at the tables, covered in vinyl tablecloths, each a different color. There were only a few people there, sipping on coffee or eating a very late lunch.

"Hi, Zonta?" Someone stood behind me. I turned to face the most handsome guy I had ever seen. He was the same height as me and his face was perfect. His dark hair was neatly combed, and his wool scarf was still tightly wrapped around his neck over his black pea coat. He was obviously Emma's brother because he looked Asian American, but he didn't seem to have any of Emma's always-irritated personality. His broad, perfect smile began to waver. "You are Zonta, right?"

I awkwardly shifted. "Yes, I'm sorry." I pulled my jacket off my other shoulder so I could hold out my hand. "You must be Joseph." I felt my cheeks warm. I couldn't believe I had just stood there and stared at this pretty-boy like a starstruck girl.

"Yes, I am." That beautiful smile flashed again as he shook my hand. Both of our hands were still cold, but I didn't pull away before he did. Then I wondered if I had held it too long. What was wrong with me? "Where do you want to sit?" Joseph asked as he scanned Bence's Good Vibes.

"The corner would be perfect." I pointed at the one place in the restaurant that had a couple of colorful couches and some very large beanbags. "It will be the most private . . . I mean it should be a good place to be alone . . . I mean to study." I shook my head and growled at myself.

"Did you just growl?" Joseph was still smiling as he walked next to me toward the 70's corner.

I couldn't believe he heard that. "Yes. Sorry. Not always great with saying what I mean." He laughed. I was thankful.

We picked a very orange couch with a low coffee table in front of it big enough to hold any books we might use. "Can I get you a coffee?" Joseph asked me.

I looked up from my pile of books that I was still pulling out of my book bag. Confused, I looked at Joseph. This was not a date, although I wouldn't mind if it was. I quickly pushed that thought away and stood up. "I can't remember what they have. I'll come with you."

We left our pile of stuff on the couch, and I followed Joseph up to the counter to order. He had on a basic black sweater and blue jeans. I tried not to look too closely as I straightened out my black Hancock High sweatshirt. A huge white lightning bolt covered the back. Not my best look. I did a quick pat-down of my hair to make sure no strands were out of place. Satisfied, I tucked one hand in my back jeans pocket as I finally reached his side.

The only lava lamp in the room sat next to the cash register. Pink shapes moved around slowly, like a soothing dance. "Haven't seen one of those in a long time." Joseph smiled again. He needed to stop doing that. He looked at the menu that was written in chalk on large black-boards stuck to the wall. "I guess I'll have a large Groovy Coffee." I had forgotten how the menu was full of 70's slang. I should have taken my time picking a place to meet. I had choices. Like the public library or even the Starbucks in the center of town next to the courthouse. Why did I ever believe it was a good idea for Joseph to meet me in such a strange place? Did he think I was strange?

"The Fab Fries are good," I said awkwardly. "Better than the lunchroom. That's for sure."

"I don't miss those days in the lunchroom." His smile wavered a little.

We didn't say anything else as he bought his coffee, and I bought a small basket of Fab Fries with an ice-water to drink. I didn't want to eat too much junk food in front of him. We settled back on the couch, and he pulled out a notebook and pen. As he opened it, he looked at me. He was getting down to business. "So where do you think you need the most help?"

I took a sip of my ice-water and put it down slowly like I was really thinking about his question. "I really am not too sure." He didn't say anything but waited for me to explain. So I did. "I feel like I understand most of the subjects, but then I get easily confused when I look at the practice questions." Joseph wrote down what I was saying. He had me give him examples of what I meant. I showed him, as he continued to take notes. After about fifty minutes of me going over all my sticky notes and dog-eared pages in my SAT study guide, he stopped writing.

"Sounds like we really need to focus on test-taking." He smiled. I was happy to see that smile again.

"Isn't that what you are here for?" I tried to sound like I was teasing, but I was serious.

Joseph frowned, briefly, but then smiled again. "Yes, you are right. However, it seems you are confident in the subjects, but need to work on understanding *how* to take the test."

"That makes sense." I smiled.

"But we will still cover subjects as well. That way I can see what you really do know." Joseph started to put away his notebook.

"Well," I began and then stopped to wait until he was paying attention. "You may be disappointed in what I don't know."

Joseph's eyebrows rose. "Disappointing or not disappointing me is *not* the goal." He cocked his head to the side. His smile was gone. "Right?"

I felt my cheeks warm again. "Right."

He stood up to leave but stopped to look down at me. He clearly was not a high school teen and I very much felt like a child. "Listen, Zonta." He was very serious. "For this to work you have got to do this for you. *Not* for me."

"I know," I said very quickly. "I was just . . ." I didn't know what I was, so I didn't finish the sentence.

Joseph let that smile slowly return. "For what it's worth. From what you've shown me, you won't be a disappointment . . . to anyone."

Chapter 24

Silvia

"Joe? Is that you?" Silvia Hemby's voice took me by surprise. I had already started packing my books back into my bag when I looked up. Silvia had blocked Joseph's path as he headed toward the door. I could only see the back of his head, but his whole body went very rigid as Silvia approached him. I couldn't help but stare as Silvia reached out and rustled Josephs perfect hair. "I haven't seen you since last May. You didn't return any of my texts." She was a little taller than Joseph, mostly because she had on some boots with crazy heels. A very snug winter jacket made sure everyone could see how beautiful and classy she was, even in the middle of winter.

"Hi, Silvia." I could barely hear Joseph respond. "Been busy."

"I heard you got into Hemby University." She reached out to touch his arm. He took a step back. She ignored his move and took a step toward him. "Good for you. I'm sure your parents are *sooo* proud of their son getting into one of the country's top business schools."

When Joseph didn't respond to her, Silvia's eyes grew wide with an idea. "Oh, Joe, you have got to join me and my friends. We're meeting at my place right now. They would love to meet you! A college boy and all. I talk about you all the time! I just came in here to get a large order of Fab Fries to go."

"No thanks, Silvia." Joseph was very calm.

Silvia frowned. "Come on, Joe. You have ignored me for too long." She thought for a second. "If you come with me then I will make sure my parents place a huge order with Tang-Lee Fabrics."

"I really cannot come to your house, Silvia." Joseph remained calm. But I was not. I felt my cheeks begin to burn. What was she doing?

Silvia had not spotted me yet, but I was already walking toward them. I got close enough to hear her quietly, but firmly, add, "But if you don't come, I will make sure that Tang-Lee Fabrics loses my parents' orders."

I almost screamed at Silvia. Since when had Silvia turned into a jerk? I knew that look on her face! It was the same look on Carlos's face when he gripped my hand. He was going to get what he wanted. Was Silvia like Carlos?

I calmed myself as I walked up right behind Joseph. Silvia still hadn't seen me. Her face was so close to Joseph and her focus so intense. She didn't care who was around her. I took a deep breath and tapped

Joseph on the shoulder. He turned around and faced me. It was not the same Joseph I had talked to only a few minutes earlier. His hair was still messed up and his face was stone cold. Although his anger was clearly simmering, he remained calm.

Before he could say anything, I smiled really big and said, "Did I hear Silvia call you Joe? Are you Joseph Tang-Lee?" I took a quick breath and rambled on. "I hope so because I really need us to get started on our lesson. You promised to tutor me for an hour. So I'm ready when you are." Then I smiled. Like the sweet, nice girl I knew how to be. But at that moment, I felt a little shift. I hadn't felt like I *had* to act nice to make others feel good about themselves. I was using it as a tool. A tool to protect Joseph. It was strange, but it felt great. The look on Silvia's face told me she believed me. And why shouldn't she? It was who I had always been to her. Nice and sweet.

Joseph took only a second to respond. "Yes, you must be Zonta." He turned to Silvia. "I really need to get to my tutoring." He didn't dismiss her, though. "You understand, right?"

Silvia's face looked a little surprised as she took in my sweatshirt and blue jeans. "Hi, Zonta."

"Hey, Silvia." I smiled. "Did I mess up something?" I looked as dumb as I could. She was used to me being clueless, so it wasn't hard.

"No, no. Totally okay." Silvia faked her best smile. She looked at Joseph again as if trying to figure out his game. She let her eyes take in all of him, like Carlos had done to me. Silvia whispered, "Too bad, my Joey-pie." She reached in and kissed his cheek. "I really do miss you."

My eyes grew wide, and I took a step back. I felt myself begin to shake. But Joseph stood stone faced and clearly did not enjoy the kiss. He nodded at Silvia. "Got to go." He finally dismissed her.

Joseph followed me to the orange couch where I began to unpack the books from my bag back onto the coffee table. He did the same. He did not look up to see if Silvia had left. But I did. I was shaking, but still holding onto my nice-girl act. I smiled at her as she took another glance in our direction. Then she walked out the door with a to-go box of Fab Fries. She did not smile back.

Chapter 25

Joey-pie

"She's gone." I said and stopped organizing my books. I was still shaking. Why would Silvia treat Joseph that way? Like Carlos treated me. He leaned back on the couch, took a deep breath, and closed his eyes. I had to ask, "What was that all about?"

Joseph didn't answer at first. So I waited. I didn't start to pack up anything just in case she came back. I decided to lean back against the couch too and calm myself down. I looked out over the restaurant and saw that the early dinner crowd was beginning to arrive. A few people greeted each other and started laughing. One older man came in with what looked like a granddaughter. He pointed at the lava lamp and the little girl giggled with joy.

"I was a senior at Hancock High when Silvia was a junior." Joseph started. I looked over at him, but he was still leaning against the couch with his eyes closed. So I leaned back again and watched the little girl stare at the lava lamp. Joseph continued, "She had the biggest crush on me and was determined to date me. But I was not into her. At all."

I turned to face him. Even with his eyes closed I preferred to look at him. Mostly because I wanted to make sure I could hear what he had to say. Joseph shook his head, eyes still closed. "But Silvia was so determined to get me. She told everyone she would get her some Joey-pie."

"Ew!" I couldn't help myself. This was not the Silvia that I knew. She was someone I wanted to be like. Popular. Well liked. Kind to everyone. Then I remembered my Christmas party. There was a part of Silvia I did not know at all. She liked to party. She liked what came with partying. I was beginning to understand why I was never invited to any of her parties. But I never would have thought she'd be a creep like Carlos.

Joseph finally opened his eyes and looked at me. He saw the raw disgust on my face and smirked. "Yes, I agree." Then he looked away again. "But as much as I tried to stay away, she kept trying to find a way. Then, finally, she did."

"Through your parents." I guessed.

Joseph nodded and looked at me again. "Yes. She found out her parents were customers of Tang-Lee Fabrics and then begged her mom to ask my mother if I could tutor her."

"You were her tutor?" I frowned. But then, all of a sudden, I made the connection. "That's where my mom got your number! From Mrs. Hemby, Silvia's mom! Makes sense now."

Joseph sighed. "I didn't want to tutor her, but my parents convinced me that it was good for business. So I did it." He shook his head. "But it was awful. Every week she tried to hit on me. She'd touch my knee or my thigh. She'd reach over and peck me on my cheek. A few times she tried to grab me . . . well . . . you can guess where."

I thought I was going to be sick. "That's awful!" Would Carlos try to touch more than my hand? Was my hand just his first move?

"I tried to stop tutoring her since she didn't want to study anyway. But when I told my parents she was assaulting me, they told me that it was ridiculous and that I better never mention it to anyone. Ever. They were so afraid that if I said something the scenario would be turned on to me. I would be accused of assaulting her."

"So how did you get out of it?" I asked.

"I told her *no* every time. But she kept on assaulting me. I needed a better plan. I thought she might be less obvious in public. So I asked to meet at coffee shops or somewhere besides her house. She didn't like it. But her parents didn't argue, and told her it was a good idea to get out of the house. Turns out, two times tutoring at the library was enough for her. She didn't want to be seen being tutored. I quickly realized she was ashamed of being tutored. Then, a few months later, I graduated and focused on starting at Hemby University. I finally had some peace."

"Until today?"

He nodded. "Until today."

"But she ended up backing off. Even though she threatened you at first."

"She did back off. After that nasty kiss." He shook off the memory and finally patted down his ruffled hair. Then he looked me straight in my eyes. No smile. No frown. No cold stare. Just Joseph. "Because of you."

I shook my head. "I didn't do . . ."

"Yes, you did." He reached to grab my hand, but quickly backed off and settled for placing his hand flat down on the couch cushion next to me. "Thank you!"

I grinned. I didn't want him to leave upset. "Hey, listen. I think it's been one intense tutoring lesson. Can you promise me it won't be this intense every time?"

All of a sudden, a raw belly laugh escaped from Joseph. "I promise."

I laughed too. I suddenly had a question. "How are you tutoring me and going to Hemby University?"

"Easy. I live at home since the campus is only in Hemby. Easier to help my parents and make a little extra cash tutoring and working in the family business."

I nodded, thankful he lived at home. "One more thing." I dared to tease. "Would you prefer me to call you Joseph or Joey-pie?"

He reached out and shoved my arm. "Shut up." He smiled. "*Joseph* will do just fine."

Chapter 26

Without Ozzie

"Have you even checked on him?" Lilly was standing right in front of my face, blocking my locker. Her blond-highlighted hair began to fall into her face, so she shoved it behind both her ears. She looked pissed.

"Who? What are you talking about?" I tried to get her to move so I could grab the books I needed for first period. The weekend had been calm and I did a whole lot of thinking about Joseph. I couldn't wait for Tuesday. I had texted Vonny all weekend and gave her every detail of Joseph's drama. Of course, Vonny wanted to tell me all about her family's latest adventure out west. I still couldn't remember a single detail she shared. I'm not sure either one of us really listened to each other. But it didn't really matter.

"Ozzie!" Lilly shoved her hair again behind her ears, even though not a single strand had moved. She studied my face for any sign of understanding. I frowned and then lifted my eyebrows, very confused.

Her mouth dropped open. "Are you kidding me, Zonta? Ozzie had his ACL surgery last Wednesday and you haven't even checked on him."

I suddenly remembered. "That's right, he did." I smiled. "How did it go?"

Lilly folded her arms across her chest. "You would know if you had checked on him."

I suddenly worried something had gone wrong. "Is he okay?"

Lilly stared at me for a second. "Actually, I'm not going to tell you. You'll have to ask him yourself." She finally stepped out of my way.

Instead of reaching for my locker I watched Lilly back away from me. "Seriously?" What was her problem? She was acting like I'd been a jerk to Ozzie, but I hadn't! We were just beginning to be friends. I didn't have to know every little thing he was doing. Did I?

She nodded. "Seriously!" And then she turned to head down the hall toward first period. Her old-green-camo-backpack was the last thing I saw as she turned the corner. My stomach flipped. Did Ozzie expect me to check on him? Had I missed something? What if I had? I didn't want him to be upset, so I decided I better check on him. Just in case Lilly was right.

I had to hurry, so I wouldn't be late. But still, I quickly pulled out my phone.

hi how did surgery go

I kept glancing at my phone as I grabbed my books, hoping Ozzie would text back. He did.

good

I quickly texted back.

great

Only a few seconds later he replied.

u good

Suddenly he was asking about me. I thought he would tell me more about the surgery. But he wasn't going to. That was okay with me since I needed to get to class and needed to end this quickly.

yes

k

ttyl

ttyl

And that was it. I was relieved. But why did Lilly have to scare me like that?

I made it to first period as Ms. Williams was getting her papers together. I headed to the back of the room where Lilly sat. I needed to talk to her, so I took the shortest path, which meant I had to pass Carlos and Blake. I didn't think much of it until I suddenly felt a hand graze my butt. I quickly turned and saw Carlos pretend nothing had happened, but Blake's eyes were wide and staring at Carlos too. Blake was not smiling. Carlos looked at me and gave me an innocent look. "What?"

"You know *what!*" I quietly growled. I wanted to call him an asshole, but I swallowed the word along with the sick feeling. Why couldn't I figure out how to deal with Carlos? It came easily when I was trying to help Joseph, but at that moment I was at a loss for what else to say.

A huge grin spread across Carlos's face. He got what he wanted. I didn't have time for this. He didn't deserve one more second of my time. I had to move on and make him think it didn't bother me enough to keep talking to him. As I turned to leave, I heard Blake ask Carlos. "Why did you . . .?"

"Shut up, Blake!" was all Carlos had in response. So Blake didn't say another word.

I decided the best way to shake off Carlos was to focus on my first goal. Talk to Lilly. I quickly came up to Lilly's desk where she looked up at me and acted surprised. I held out my phone and pointed at Ozzie's texts. "He's fine. The surgery was fine. There is nothing wrong. Why did you make me text him?"

Lilly shook her head and didn't even look at my phone. "I didn't make you text him."

"Yes, you did!" I glanced to the front of the room and found Ms. Williams talking to Mateo about something. So I turned back to Lilly. "You told me I had to ask him myself and made me think something was wrong."

Lilly frowned at me in disbelief. "Zonta. There *is* something wrong."

"What?" I shoved my phone in my back pocket and gripped my books against my chest waiting for her to answer.

Lilly looked up at me. Her challenging stare transformed into sadness. "You, Zonta. Why didn't you even think to check on him? Why didn't you even care to ask about the surgery until you thought something was wrong?"

I swallowed. Confused. "Why should I?"

Lilly nodded slowly. The look of pity she gave me made my stomach turn as she responded, "Because that's what friends do. But you wouldn't know that because it's all about you. Everything is about you!" She was wrong! I was nice. I cared about people. But I wasn't used to having more friends than just Vonny. If I thought it mattered to Ozzie, I would have texted him earlier. But even his texts back to me made it seem like it was no big deal. Lilly didn't know what she was talking about!

"Miss Jones, will you please have a seat?" Ms. Williams was ready to start class.

I nodded at her as I turned away from Lilly. My stomach was still hurting as I walked back to my desk, close to the front, and next to the window. I had to figure out how to show Lilly I was a good person *and* I had to stay far away from Carlos's groping hands.

How dare Lilly think that I only think of myself. After everything my family did for her. Actually, what my parents did for her. I didn't dare look back at Lilly. I didn't want her to see my face as I replayed her words over and over again. And I didn't want to look at Carlos's stares that had become more intense since . . . since . . . since Ozzie had his surgery.

Chapter 27

New Friends?

I sat down at a table close to the large wall of windows looking out over the outside patio. I wished it wasn't too cold to sit outside. It was the best way to get away from the stress and smell of school, even if the buildings still surrounded you. I looked at the "temporary classroom" trailers and wondered how long it would take for the school to build another wing. They needed get rid of the ugly boxes. I looked at the muddy mess that used to be the lawn. I hoped one day it would be green again. Maybe one day we would get to sit in the grass or toss footballs again. But I doubted it would happen anytime soon.

"Are you eating alone today?" Mary Ann pulled me away from my run-away thoughts.

I smiled up at her as she stood with her lunch tray. "Not if you're planning on eating with me." I had tried not to think of Lilly's words, or Carlos's nasty touch. But thinking about the outdoor eating area was not really working. Maybe eating lunch with Mary Ann would help.

Mary Ann nodded across the lunchroom at two black girls who nodded back at her. "Hope it's okay if my two new friends join us." She placed her tray down across from me.

"Sure." I smiled awkwardly. It was strange watching two girls, who were Mary Ann's friends, walking toward us. "I thought you didn't make friends easily?"

Mary Ann looked at me a little surprised. "I didn't say that. I said people don't always welcome me. And I don't have many old friends who will talk about old times." That was not how I understood it, but I didn't know why it mattered. I wanted to be happy for her . . . that she was making new friends. She glanced at the girls and then focused on me. "Do you know Imani and Summer?"

I shook my head as they approached. The shorter of the two was heavy-set, and she wore it well. Her dark blue jeans that hugged her body, and her low-cut v-sweater screamed *confidence*. Her hair was in an updo that boasted a crown of perfect braids. She clearly knew I was giving her the once over, but she didn't care. She gave me a wide smile and spoke without hesitation. "Hi, I'm Summer."

"Hi." I smiled back since I knew how to be polite. She then set down her lunch tray and scooted in next to me. She was so close that I could feel her shoulder touch mine off and on. I tried to scoot over a bit to give her some room, but she scooted with me.

"That's my friend, Imani." Summer pointed at Imani, who was as tall as Mary Ann, but not as skinny. Imani looked like an athlete, but I couldn't for the life of me figure out which of Hancock High's teams she was on. I smiled at Imani as she smiled shyly and pulled awkwardly at the collar of her cropped jeans jacket. Her hair was cut short and softly curled, like three small waves climbing up each cheek. Summer nudged my arm. "She doesn't talk much, but she will once you get to know her. Mary Ann has told us all about you." Summer looked me up and down and I suddenly felt self-conscious of my hair. I hadn't done anything with it for a long time except let it dry naturally and tame it with gel. I grabbed a handful and pulled it over one shoulder. "Want me to do your hair?" Summer smiled.

I hadn't said a word to her and she was already wanting to do my hair. I was a little surprised. "Well, uh . . . uh." My head started racing with thoughts of what kind of hair style she'd try.

"Give her some time, Summer." Mary Ann interrupted.

"Okay." Summer smiled and then took a bite of her meatloaf.

"Thank you for the offer." I said to Summer and then rolled my eyes at Mary Ann. "My ADHD gets in the way sometimes and it takes me a second to know what to say."

Summer turned her head and smiled again. "It really is okay. I come off as strong sometimes. But I felt I already knew you since Mary Ann told us how nice you've been to her."

I smiled and wished Lilly had heard her say that. "How did you meet Mary Ann?" I asked as I sipped my water.

"In Advanced Art." Summer answered. "That girl can draw like nobody's business!"

"Really?" I looked at Mary Ann. I didn't know that about her. Then I noticed Mary Ann's sweatshirt and it had one of Picasso's paintings on the front. A distorted image of a blond girl was looking at a reflection of herself. The reflection looked even more strange with blue or, maybe, green hair. I wasn't too sure. I should have paid closer attention to the things that Mary Ann did or wore that screamed *I am an artist*. But I hadn't.

Mary Ann shrugged. "I don't like to boast."

"Shut up," Summer teased. "You boast all the time about how you won this contest or that contest."

Mary Ann tilted her head as if she had to think about it a second, then she nodded. "True." They both started laughing. Imani smiled but was more interested in making sure her potatoes didn't touch her meat.

I spent most of lunch listening to Summer and Mary Ann talk about their art class and then by the time they mentioned the first "art college," I was looking out the wall of windows again. I didn't even know Mary Ann was some artist. She clearly thought I was her friend, but I was beginning to wonder if I was. Maybe Lilly was right. Maybe I was only nice when it mattered to me.

Chapter 28

Really?

As lunch period came to an end, Summer and Imani left, so I stood up to leave too, but Mary Ann just sat across from me, staring at me.

"What?" I asked, and then sat down again.

"Are you okay?" She tilted her head toward the large wall of windows. "Seems like you were more outside than inside with us."

I snorted. "Seems like I suck at being friends." When I saw her eyes narrow, I added, putting on my best nice-girl voice, "Sorry! If I'm so awful to be around, then you can just eat with Summer and Imani without me."

Mary Ann threw her arms in the air. "Really? Just like that you're going to pull away? Summer and Imani were so nice to you, and you ignore them *and* me for the rest of lunch. And now you act like some . . . some sad little girl who has no friends!"

"No, that's not true." I frowned. "My ADHD makes my mind wander."

"Don't use your ADHD as an excuse!" She argued back. I wanted to respond, but I couldn't. She was right. I had used it as an excuse.

Suddenly, Mary Ann stood up, but I didn't move. She looked down at me, waiting for me to say something. But I didn't even look up at her. It wasn't that I didn't want to tell her I was sorry, or that I was upset with Lilly, or that Carlos was beginning to really scare me. I just couldn't. I didn't know how. My throat was so tight, and my eyes began to burn. I was afraid if I opened my mouth, a desperate scream would escape. I couldn't be so desperate, so pitiful. Not more than I already was. So I sat and stared at the strange face of the girl on Mary Ann's sweater.

I kept waiting for her to leave. But she didn't. When I dared to finally look up at her, she was still staring at me, but a little less pissed. I still couldn't talk. So she did. "Come on. Let's go."

I frowned and cleared my throat, hoping I would hold it together. "Where?"

Mary Ann took a deep breath and put one hand on her hip. "Principles of Business and Finance." When I didn't move, she added, "Are you coming or not?" I nodded and grabbed my tray. As we walked toward the trashcans she whispered. "I'm not sure what is going on with you. But you can't get rid of me that easily."

Chapter 29

Off

"You seem off." Joseph said as we went over several math terms. Bence's Good Vibes was having a slow Tuesday. I was thankful. I needed to be in a place that only cared about good food and relaxing. Except, I was supposed to be studying. I was so tired from feeling like I was saying and doing all the wrong things. I needed something to remind me that I was okay. Not a sad little girl with no friends. Or, the object of someone's groping hands. I needed a way to reclaim that image of kind-sweet-innocent Zonta that was voted on to the homecoming court.

"I'm fine. Really." I smiled. A part of me meant it because I was sitting next to Joseph. He calmed me and made me think I'd walk away from all this unharmed. He did, for the most part. *He* moved past Silvia's harassment. So I should be able to handle Carlos's unwanted actions since they didn't seem as bad as what Joseph went through.

"Okay," Joseph responded, but I could see he didn't quite believe me. Still, he moved on to the next section in the SAT study guide. He wasn't going to push me to explain myself.

I took a sip of my Groovy Coffee and pretended that life would just work itself out.

Chapter 30

No Way!

"How's it going?" Vashon's smile was the best way to start the day. He was always happy.

I was standing in front of my locker killing as much time as possible before first period started. The less time in U.S. History without Carlos licking his lips at me, the better. Vashon was a perfect excuse to linger. "Doing okay. What do you want?" Clearly, he was not just checking on me. I knew he was up to something.

"I'm deeply hurt. Can't a man ask you how you're doing?" He gripped his shirt with one hand, faking a heart attack. But his smile only grew.

I raised my eyebrows. "Really?" I giggled at his silly hurt look.

Vashon suddenly waved one hand in the air. "Okay. Okay. You're right." He smiled again and came in closer. "So are you going to Owen Hemby's rager this Friday?"

I scrunched up my face. "Ew! Absolutely not!"

Vashon's smile dropped. "What? Why?" He looked down the hall and back before he whispered, "I was hoping I could catch a ride with you."

As much as I wanted to say yes and make Vashon's day, I just couldn't. I knew Carlos would be at Owen's party, since they were friends. Which meant there was no way I would go. "Not a chance. Don't think your granny would be too happy with you at a huge party."

Vashon sucked air through his teeth. "What she doesn't know won't hurt her."

"Get to class!" Mr. Soza was making his morning rounds through the halls. He waved his broom handle at us. "Don't be late!" Then he gave us his classic smile, placed the broom onto his bright yellow cleaning cart, loaded his arms with some paper towels and disappeared into the boys' bathroom. As soon as the door closed, about three boys came hurrying out. Mr. Soza's voice still followed them. "You better not be late!"

Vashon and I both laughed as the boys ran past us, one still zipping up his pants. Then I looked at Vashon who gave me his puppy-dog eyes, begging me one last time. I sighed and shook my head. "No! You'll have to find someone else to take you. I want to stay as far away from that party as possible. Since it's Owen's party then Chastity and

Silvia will be there . . . and I'm guessing Carlos and Blake will be there. So I *won't* be there!"

Vashon tilted his head. "Hmmmmm." He scratched his chin dramatically. "Seems you have a long list of people to avoid." Then he slung his arm around my neck and whispered. "Promise me you won't put me on your list?"

I laughed and shoved his arm off me. "Not a chance!" The bell rang and everyone was emptying the halls. We needed to get going too, so I pointed a finger into his face and tried not to giggle as I growled. "But don't mess with me or I might put you at the top."

Vashon started backing away pretending to be afraid. I laughed as I watched him dramatically disappear into a classroom. I turned to finally head toward first period. But suddenly, my stomach flipped. Carlos and Blake were standing in front of me.

Chapter 31

Hard Press

"What's so funny?" Carlos was only standing a foot away. Blake was next to him, smiling at me. I'd have to go around them to get to my classroom. In any case, we'd all be late if we waited any longer.

"Nothing." I said as I looked down and tried to move past Carlos.

But he stepped in front of me. "Why can't you laugh for me like you did for that freshman?"

I frowned, but I still didn't look up at him. Did he not see that his way of flirting was just creepy? I decided the best way to get rid of him was to pretend he didn't exist. That was still better than being ugly to him. So I tried to move again. This time Carlos came in closer. Quickly, he stretched out his arms to lean against my locker, trapping me between them. He gently touched the back of my left hand as I gripped my books. There he was again, touching my hand. I should have never sent him that pic!

My heart raced as my disgust for Carlos turned to fear. I tried to duck under his arms, but he wouldn't let me as he pushed me up against the locker with his whole body. My face was at his chest and I thought I was going to gag from the overwhelming musty smell. Couldn't tell if it was his deo or pot. All I knew was I had to get away.

There were no kind or nice words. No leaving on a good note. No trying *not* to be ugly. As my fear grew, I felt something in me shift. I was done. "Get off of me!" I growled. I shoved him, but he was too big.

"I think you really like me, Zonta." His mouth was right at my hair line and his breath was warm against my forehead. "You look so hot in purple!" One hand gently touched the hem of my favorite long-sleeve shirt.

Fear consumed me, but I didn't scream. I thought maybe I could insult him, and he'd loosen his grip. "You need some mouth wash! Get off me before I gag." I pushed again.

I could hear Blake laugh, but it was strained. "*She* told you! Now let's go."

"Shut up, Blake!" Carlos said without moving away from me. This time he inched in and I felt my breath squeezed out of me. His body was pressed so closely that I felt a panic set in. Every part of me that had wanted to deal with him on my own and make it all go away, was gone. I finally began to scream.

"Let's go!" Blake grabbed Carlos's arm and pulled him. "She doesn't want to play along with you. So let's go."

Carlos backed off as I screamed again. Louder. Longer. I couldn't stop. Not until the nearest classroom door opened and a teacher ran out at the same time Mr. Soza shot through the boys' bathroom door into the hall. But Carlos and Blake were already gone.

Chapter 32

Accident?

"Carlos said it was an accident." Ms. Nazari stared at me from across her desk. Her straight, jet-black hair curved around her face, stopping at her jaw line. Bright red lipstick and matching, red-rimmed glasses, only made her look more like a professional therapist, rather than our school's guidance counselor. Principal Ketner had quickly shoved the "incident" into Ms. Nazari's hands: not a big enough issue for her to deal with personally. Reality was, we all knew Mrs. Ketner was counting her days until retirement.

"But it wasn't an accident!" I wiped my face with the back of my very-wet-sleeve of my purple shirt. It was soaked from thirty minutes of crying, off and on. I kept trying to pull it together, but something was beginning to break inside of me. "You can ask Blake. He was there."

Ms. Nazari reached into one of her drawers and then pulled out a box of tissues. She handed it to me. I took it and grabbed a handful.

As she watched me, she put on her best I-feel-for-you look. But the words that followed did not match. "Carlos already told us that he tripped as he hurried to class. He fell up against you and then you panicked."

"Did you even ask Blake?" I challenged her as I set the box down on her desk, with a little more force than I should have.

She looked at the box for a moment. "Listen, Zonta. I do not think we need to bring Blake into this."

"Why not?" I raised my voice. "He's the one who sees everything Carlos does to me. He even saw him grab my butt."

Ms. Nazari raised her eyebrows. "He touched your bottom? And he has been making other advances?"

I nodded. "Yes. He's freaking me out."

Ms. Nazari nodded her head calmly and smiled gently. "I think, Zonta, that you are overreacting to Carlos who appears to have a crush on you."

My mouth dropped open. "What?"

"He told me . . ." The school counselor leaned in as if she had a secret to share, ". . . that he likes you very much and may be showing his affection for you too openly. He said you two have even texted each other."

"One time!" I started to raise my voice.

"But you sent him a pic, right?" Ms. Nazari asked.

I shook my head. "Are you kidding me?" I wanted to scream and cry at the same time. Was she blaming me for Carlos's actions? "It was a stupid pic of the back of my hand to get him to stop texting me!"

She smiled. "I think you should embrace this time in your life where teen love is so fierce. So passionate . . . So . . ."

"Please stop!" I interrupted her crazy notion of teen love. "I don't care what he said he *feels*. I care about what he *did* to me. What he still might do."

"I wouldn't worry about that." She tilted her head slightly. "I told him he needs to stay away from you since you do not feel the same way about him. And he promised he would."

"Promised?" My mouth dropped again. "Promised? Really?"

Ms. Nazari stood up and came around her desk to walk me out. She was ready to move on to the next Hancock High crisis. I stood up too, still shocked. Just before she opened her door she added. "Trust me. Everything will be okay. Carlos is just figuring out how to act around girls he likes. It just takes some guys a little longer."

"Well then he better learn fast." I almost vomited as I left her office, passing two freshman boys with hall passes in their hands and scowls on their faces.

That was it. I had to go back to class. I had to pretend Carlos was a pathetic, innocent boy crushing on me. But I was already tired of being nice and moving on *and* making excuses for Carlos's actions. I was more than tired. I just couldn't do it anymore. I couldn't walk back into class and pretend. Instead, I headed to the girls' bathroom.

Chapter 33

In the Toilet

I was shaking as I locked myself in the cleanest stall. I had to find someone who could help me. Someone who knew what a creep Carlos really was. Leaning my forehead against the cold metal door I pulled out my phone.

Ozzie r u up?

It was 10 am and I knew that he liked to sleep late.

Zonta? r u not at school?

im at school. in bathroom.

Okay good to know u think about me when u need to go 

I wanted to scream. What was I doing? He must have thought I was a freak. But I needed to talk to someone.

very funny 😜 *needed to get out of class. how r u*

fine. knee hurts like hell

sorry about that

its all good. getting better each day

when r u back at school

He couldn't get back fast enough. Carlos kept his distance from me when Ozzie was around. I never really noticed before. But now . . .

looks like next wed IF i keep moving and getting better

great

I didn't know what else to say. But I didn't want to stop texting. Not yet. I needed him to help me. But how could he when he wasn't at school? I was relieved to see Ozzie send the next message.

u okay

I wasn't sure what to say. How could I even begin to explain this? I didn't want to worry him. So I lied.

yes

good

My stomach turned again. I shoved my phone onto the toilet paper holder and puked full force into the toilet. I was shaking as I picked up my phone again. I couldn't pretend. Not anymore.

Actually no. carlos is being an ass

like always

worse

just ignore him

hard to do

tell him ill whoop his ass if he touches u

too late

what

just pressed his whole-self up against me in the hall. said it was an accident. Ms. Nazari believes him.

so sorry

I felt my tears return. Ozzie was on the other side of Hancock, not down the hall. And he was on crutches . . . again. When I didn't respond, Ozzie did.

kick him next time

i tried to shove him. he was too big

Suddenly my phone rang. It was Ozzie.

"Ozzie?" I whispered. As far as I knew I was alone in the girls' bathroom.

"Zonta. You listen to me. If I was there right now, I would beat the hell out of Carlos. Even with my crutches." I let out a small sob. "I think you need to get out of there and come see me NOW. I'll teach you how to handle Carlos."

Chapter 34

Defense

I left school. Told them I had puked. Which I had. I ran to my car. I felt like Carlos was around every corner and behind each parked car. But he wasn't. I locked every door to my little blue Honda Civic as soon as I got into it.

Within twenty minutes I was in the Hall neighborhood. Only moments later, I was pulling up to Ozzie's house. Last time I had been there, Lilly, Vashon, and I were afraid Ozzie had killed himself. I remembered the cop cars parked outside while we waited, standing in the driveway, to hear if Ozzie was okay or not. Then there was the relief we all felt when Officer Evans asked us to come inside and talk to Ozzie. Of course, at the time, I was still pissed at Ozzie for how he treated me, even though I was relieved he wasn't hurt. All that happened only six weeks earlier, but it felt like a lifetime ago.

The memory quickly faded as I walked up to the front door. Ozzie was already standing there, straining on his crutches, waiting for me. His Browns cap was turned around backwards and the look on his face showed me he was ready to help me fight back. I embraced his neck and sobbed. He patted me briefly, trying not to fall over from my weight and his. "Trust me, Zonta." He closed the door behind us as we stepped into his living room. "I know Carlos better than most people."

"But why won't the adults believe me?" I was furious.

"Because he knows how to say the things they want to hear." Ozzie's look was intense. He was pissed too! "So until others believe you, let me show you some things."

And he did. I learned that trying not to look at Carlos and turning my head, or backing away from him, only made things worse. I left myself wide open. I needed to be ready in case he ever tried again. I needed to always know where he was *and* where his hands were, so I could avoid them or stop them from reaching me.

I learned that talking trash back to Carlos only made him think I was flirting. Made him think I liked to play rough. I needed to tell him *no* or to *back off* and move on. I should never let him get into it with me. And no texting. At all! Block him off any social media. And if he comes at me, I should *not* wait to react. I should kick or use my arms and hit him. Even between the legs if it gets him to back off. Then get out of there. But if I can't get away, I should scream sooner and louder and keep hitting him in every place that would hurt. Like poking his eyes or hitting his ears hard. Any sensitive part of his body is worth aiming for, like his neck. I didn't have to be a martial arts expert, just do something, and then run like hell.

The biggest thing was that I should keep away from him in the first place. If I see him coming, I should never wait to see what happens. Just move. Just go. Don't give him an opportunity.

"But I have to see him at school," I argued.

"Yes, but don't be alone in the hall," he argued back. "Always be where there are other people."

After an hour of talking and me showing him some of the moves he described, I felt a little more in control. He made me promise to think about and practice what I had learned. "Thanks, Ozzie." I smiled.

He grinned back. "That's what friends are for."

I dropped my eyes and said, "I'm sorry."

"For what?" Ozzie asked. I looked up and saw he was confused.

"That I didn't check on you when you had your surgery."

Ozzie chuckled. "I didn't think about it at all. It's only been a week." Then he saw the frown on my face. "Why would I expect you to check on me?"

I dropped my eyes again. "Lilly was mad at me because I hadn't checked on you."

Ozzie shook his head still chuckling. "You girls are crazy! That Lilly has sure messed with your head. She must really care about you."

"What?"

Ozzie shrugged. "Well, from my experience, the more she cares about someone, the more she gets pissed at them until they do things her way." He looked at me with wide eyes. "Trust me, I would know."

Suddenly the biggest laugh burst from deep inside. Ozzie and I laughed for a full minute before I pulled myself together again. I wiped my cheeks again with my still-wet sleeve. This time the tears were worth it.

Chapter 35

Trust

"You want a sandwich?" Ozzie asked. I had stayed with Ozzie all morning watching TV. I didn't want to go home yet and there was no way I was going back to school.

"Sure." I jumped up off the big recliner with the best view of the TV. Ozzie told me I was lucky his dad was working or else I'd have to settle for the floor, since he wasn't sharing the couch. I followed him as he easily swung on his crutches into the kitchen.

He settled at the kitchen table and propped up his leg. "Okay, since you're here you can make me some lunch." A huge grin spread across his face as he waited for me to respond.

I narrowed my eyebrows and sucked air through my teeth. "I don't think so!"

Ozzie folded his hands on the table in front of him. "I thought you would be happy to help a poor boy on crutches. Are you really that heartless?"

I rolled my eyes and teased back. "I think you *need* the practice. How will you ever improve if I help you?"

Ozzie shook his head, still holding the fake look of concern. "Well, well. See if you get any advice from me in the future!"

"Grrrr." He had me.

"Did you just growl?" Ozzie started laughing.

"Maybe." I smiled and laughed as well. "Looks like you won." I headed toward a random cabinet and opened it. But I only faced spices. "But it may take a while since I have no clue where anything is."

"Okay, okay." Ozzie stood up and swung himself toward the cabinet closest to him. "But you have to help." I nodded as he pointed out where everything was, and I hauled it all to the counter and made us each a ham and cheese sandwich. When we sat back down at the table, my stomach growled. Ozzie laughed again. "Looks like all parts of you are growling."

I smiled as I took a bite of my sandwich. We both ate and laughed. After a few minutes, memory of that day in December came back to me. I had thought about it earlier that morning, but it had never crossed my mind to bring it up. "Ozzie, can I ask you a serious question?"

Ozzie looked up from his sandwich and his smile faded. "Okay." He put his sandwich down on the plate and waited. He knew what I was going to ask.

"Why did you . . ." I saw a sadness pour over Ozzie. "Never mind. None of my business." I took a bite of the sandwich again and mumbled, "Great sandwich."

"Why did I want to kill myself?" Ozzie asked the question for me.

The bite was suddenly hard to swallow. "You don't have to say anything. Really. I'm sorry I—"

"Zonta, it's okay. I—"

"No, not really." I stopped him. "It doesn't matter if I understand or not."

"It does now." Ozzie said. I thought I saw a hint of a smile.

"Why?" I asked, confused.

"Because you trust me again. No reason for me not to trust you." He said what I had been feeling. He was right. I hadn't wanted to forgive him or even like him again. But it happened without either one of us trying. I caught myself. The truth was that *he* had been trying. At that moment I knew we had finally *both* moved on. I leaned in as Ozzie began to explain. "Zonta, I thought I didn't matter and that I didn't deserve to live."

"But you have a great family, and you're great at football. And every girl out there would love to date you," I argued. Then stopped. "Sorry. Go on."

Ozzie didn't get upset with me, instead he took a deep breath and continued. "That's what everyone saw. But not me. I saw how I hurt you and Lilly and how I didn't stand up for Blake. Then there's the fact that I may never play football again."

"But your leg will be better by next season. I'm sure—"

"No. Listen! I don't know if I even *want* to play football." Ozzie looked at his sandwich. "It has always been my family's dream. Not mine."

I understood what it meant for your family to expect you to be someone you are not meant to be. I could imagine how much worse it was for Ozzie since he was already such a football star. He felt trapped. "I'm so sorry."

Ozzie looked up at me. "For what?"

"For not even noticing. I even dated you and didn't have a clue." I shook my head. "Maybe if I had tried to be your friend first, I might have noticed sooner."

Ozzie shook his head. "Maybe, but I was pretty good at lying to everyone. Including myself."

"Are you better?" I dared ask.

Ozzie nodded. "I'm getting there. I go to counseling and my family is trying to figure it all out with me. It's weird." He smiled. "Nothing like a bunch of Waxman's trying to figure out how to talk to each other." He picked up his sandwich and then added, "I'm learning to do the things I want to do and be with the people I want to be with. AND not putting up with stuff that I don't agree with. It's a change. But I think a good one." Then he chomped down on the ham and cheese sandwich like it was the best thing he'd ever eaten.

As I sat in that kitchen with Ozzie and we moved on to talk about other things, I laughed at myself. Back in the fall it had been so important for me to be liked by Ozzie, the only boy who had been nice to me. I thought I wanted a relationship. But looking at him then, I realized it was the start of our amazing friendship.

Chapter 36

Good Vibes

A cold January rain was falling, making Bence's Good Vibes feel cozy. A round, brown throw rug had been added under the low coffee table next to our orange couch. It helped soften the feel of the study space that Joseph and I had clearly claimed as our own. We were pretty much finished, but heading out into the icy cold rain, was not something I looked forward to. So instead, I shoved off my shoes and tucked my feet under my legs as I settled deeper into the couch. Joseph looked like he wasn't ready to leave yet either. It had only been my third tutoring session, but I already dreaded the day when our sessions were no longer needed. They were some of the few times during the week when I felt safe, and myself.

"Are you ready to tell me?" Joseph closed his notebook and looked at me.

I frowned. "Tell you what?"

He took a moment to shove the notebook into his backpack and then leaned back on the couch. He closed his eyes again, like he did that day Silvia had been here. "About what's going on with you?"

He didn't look at me. So I didn't have to worry about him seeing the confused look on my face. He let me think through what I wanted to share with him, and I wasn't sure I wanted to say anything. I didn't want the peaceful moment to be ruined. Finally, I asked calmly. "Can you be more specific?" What if he was just asking about my thoughts on SAT prep? Maybe it had nothing to do with the drama at school. Maybe.

He turned his head toward me and opened his eyes. "My sister told me there was a rumor going around that some guy assaulted you." I forgot that Emma was in my first period. Of course she would have paid attention to both Carlos and me heading to the office the day before. "Is it true?"

I pulled my knees in close to my chest and nodded. "Except the school counselor believes Carlos just doesn't know how to show his feelings toward me, and that he won't act this way anymore."

Joseph sat up, pulled one knee up onto the couch so he could face me. "Do you believe his story?"

I gripped my knees tighter and shook my head. "No, because he doesn't know when to stop."

"What did your parents say?" He asked. I dropped my eyes. "You haven't told them, have you?"

"Well, sort of." I explained, "The school told them their version, or more like Carlos's version. So when I tried to go into details at dinner, they told me to just stay away from *boys-like-him*. Then they said that there are *boys-like-him* everywhere and I had to learn to deal with them. *Then* they hugged me and headed off to do the dishes."

A dark look spread across Joseph's face, and I could tell he was remembering the lack of control he felt against Silvia. "This is *not* okay, Zonta."

I loosened my grip around my knees a little and tried to sound more cheerful. "At least my friend Ozzie showed me some self-defense moves. I know a little more on how to handle Carlos if he comes across me again."

Joseph nodded, but his smile was weak. "That's good to hear." We sat in silence for a few awkward moments before he added, "If you ever need anything just call me." I couldn't tell if he was blushing or not, but he shifted his knee back down to turn away from me again. A little flutter began deep in my stomach, and I couldn't help but let a smile spread across my face. He glanced at me. "What are you smiling at?" He tried to hold onto his concerned-adult look.

I shook my head, still smiling. "I think it's very sweet of you. That's all."

He cleared his throat and explained, "I'm not trying to be sweet. I'm only concerned." Then he glanced sideways at me to see if I bought it.

I nodded but kept smiling. "If you say so."

He stood up. "I better go." He grabbed his bag to leave. "I'll see you Tuesday."

My smile softened. "Joseph." He stopped moving and looked down at me. "Thanks."

Joseph nodded but kept himself serious. "You're welcome." He turned to leave, but quickly turned back toward me one last time. "I'm glad you're able to smile. Don't let this go on much longer or you may not smile quite as easily." It was not what I expected to hear. But it was *his* truth. He didn't want it to be *mine*. He waited a moment to see it register in my eyes. My smile faded and I nodded. I saw relief in his eyes before he finally turned to go.

Chapter 37
Favor

"Zonta?" Mom's voice woke me up from my after-school nap. I had made it through Friday at Hancock High with no issues. Everything felt like a normal school day. Carlos didn't even look my way. At least that was what I observed, since I *did* look at him every so often, like Ozzie taught me. I knew where he sat and how he moved *and* was happy to see him act like I didn't exist. Maybe Ms. Nazari was right? Maybe I had misunderstood the creep. But I was not going to let my guard down. Still, the whole week had exhausted me. So when I got home, I threw on some grey sweats and a loose blue sweatshirt and collapsed on my bed.

"ZONTA!" Mom's voice grew louder, causing me to sit up. I looked at my phone and saw it was almost 6 p.m. I had slept over two hours.

"WHAT?" I screamed. And then flopped back down onto my pillow.

I could hear Mom quickly walk down the hall and open my door. She gave me the once over and put one hand on her hip. "Aren't you going to Owen Hemby's party?"

I grabbed my blankets and pulled them up to my chin. "Not a chance!" Then I frowned and sat up. "Mom! How do you know about this party? Wait . . . why do you even care?" I was so confused.

Mom sighed and came to sit next to me on my bed. "Well, Cindy just called me."

"And?" I dreaded what she was getting ready to tell me. Mrs. Hemby, Silvia's mom, had a way of getting people to do things for her.

Mom smiled. I could tell she was trying to pick her words carefully. "She asked if you were going to the party because Silvia's car is in the shop and Cindy and her husband are out of town. So she needs a ride."

My stomach turned. "Please tell me you did NOT say I would give her a ride!"

Mom scrunched up her face. "I did."

"Mom! I am not going to go to the party. Have her order a ride online or better yet, *you* take her!" I flung myself back onto my pillow and pulled up my covers again. I wasn't even trying to be nice. I was done. And as strange as it was, a part of me felt good. Free.

Mom waited a moment and then she reached out and tugged on my covers until I looked at her again. "It's not that simple." She sighed. "You see, Cindy said Silvia has been going through some things lately." I rolled my eyes. "Seriously, Zonta. Be nice! Cindy thinks she may be making some poor choices and would like you to go along and keep an eye on her."

I shot up in bed. "Are you serious? Mom! Silvia is a senior and is the queen of partying and you want me, a junior, and clearly not someone she respects, to go babysit her?" I shook my head. "Why don't they just tell her she can't go to the party. Seems logical."

Mom frowned with concern. But, clearly, not concern for me. "Owen Hemby is a distant cousin and the party is on the lake at one of the oldest Hemby estates in Hancock and all of Midway County." That meant Owen Hemby was rich. I would have never guessed. Owen Hemby lived on Lake Drive *and* he went to Hancock High, not some private school. I almost laughed.

"So what does that have to do with anything?" I asked.

Mom rubbed her neck. "It seems that Cindy wants to make sure they support the Hemby family. Not letting Silvia go would look bad." I kept looking at her in total disbelief. She grabbed my hand. "Zonta, the Hembys have influence is the county. They are one of the old families that go way back to the founding of the county." She shook her head. "I don't understand how it all works. But I need you to do me this favor and take her."

"So let me get this right. Mrs. Hemby doesn't want to upset the rich Hemby family and you don't want to upset the across-the-street Hembys?" I shook my head.

Mom started to chuckle. "When you put it that way, it sounds bad."

"It is bad, Mom!"

"I guess it is in a way, but I don't want to have issues with my neighbor. It will also be a good way for you and Silvia to get closer." She wasn't giving up. "Where is my sweet and kind Zonta? You used to jump at the opportunity to help. You always smiled and no one was *ever* your enemy."

"But no one was *really* my friend either. Except Vonny." I had to get Mom to understand. So before she could say anything, I added, "Then, when Vonny left, I quickly learned that all those smiles and being kind and sweet didn't really mean I actually had more friends. And, believe me, Silvia is NOT a friend."

Mom smiled, that sickly my-poor-baby smile. "So this would be perfect time to work on those new friendships."

That was it! I was done. "I don't want to go, Mom. Carlos might be there." I needed to wake her up from this crazy plan.

Mom considered my statement long enough for me to think she was finally going to back off. I was not that lucky. "Maybe it will be good for you to learn how to keep your distance from boys like him."

My mouth dropped. "Really? You think it's that easy?"

She looked at me. "When I was growing up, I had to learn to deal with so many creeps. I can't tell you how many times I had to slap away groping hands. I think I keep you too protected. You need to deal with the real world. This won't be the first crush you'll have to fight off." I wondered if Dad would have supported her reasoning. I didn't think Mom completely understood what she was saying. She needed to please Mrs. Hemby and she would justify her thinking, no matter what I said.

So I got out of bed. Threw on my blue jeans and shoved my feet into some old Adidas. I left my loose blue sweatshirt on and pulled my hair back in a tight ponytail. I didn't even look in the mirror. I didn't care.

I grabbed my car keys along with Dad's bulky green winter jacket that hung on me like a thick tent. On my way out the door I texted Silvia to meet me at my car.

Chapter 38

The Ride

"I see you dressed up." Silvia teased. I didn't even look at her or answer her. I just stared at the road ahead of me. There wasn't one drop of nice Zonta left in me. The rain from Thursday had turned most of the leftover snow into mush. Any freezing temps would turn the streets into nasty chunks of ice. I ended up behind a truck spewing a salt and sand mixture, slowing me down to a crawl along Seaberg Avenue. After a few more minutes, Silvia tried again. "Sorry to drag you into this."

That time I glanced at her briefly and could see she was trying to be real. "I did *not* want to go to this party. But Mom went on about all this Hemby family junk. So I guess, as a Jones, I don't have much of a say. We do the bidding of the Hembys."

Silvia laughed. "You are so lucky you aren't a Hemby."

"I can't argue that!" I snorted. "I wouldn't want to be you or Owen."

"Thanks a lot." Silvia actually sounded hurt. I frowned. This conversation was not going well. I hoped the truck would turn left onto Main Street and let me pick up speed as I continued north. The faster there, the less time to talk. Silvia grunted, "Are you really not going to apologize?"

"For what? Speaking the truth?" I didn't look at her. Turn truck. Turn!

"I used to think you were a nice person, but now I don't know," she whined.

Instead of feeling hurt, I just laughed. "Are you really saying this to me as I drive you to a party that I don't want to go to so that you and your family feel good about yourselves?"

Silvia was quiet. My heart sank when the truck did not turn onto Main Street. I'd have to follow it all the way until I could turn right onto Otis Avenue, which was a straight shot to Lake Drive. Silvia would have to show me which house was Owen's. I didn't have a clue. But if I was lucky, she wouldn't say a word until we reached the lake. I wasn't that lucky. "You know my dad is black and my mom is white."

"So? My mom is black and my dad is white." I snorted. Why were we stating facts that we both already knew? After all those years, was that suddenly the moment we were to bond because we were both biracial? Not a chance.

"Listen. Okay?" Silvia was trying to be serious.

"Alright. Go on." I took a deep breath. Silvia was quiet long enough that I turned my head for a second. She was staring at me. I quickly looked at the road again. "What? I thought you were going to tell me something!"

"Never mind. You wouldn't understand." She snorted. "You have no idea what it is like when your great grandfather was biracial when the word *biracial* wasn't even used."

"What?" I felt myself fume. She didn't know anything about my family's history, and once again, was making *her* family's drama something we needed to respect. Like the Hembys were royalty. We finally turned right onto Otis Avenue. I couldn't wait to get her out of my car.

"Look, Zonta. Owen and I are cousins that go way back. I'm just one small part of all sorts of twisted Hemby and Hancock family drama." I looked at her as she waved for me to take a right onto Lake Drive.

"So what? Does it really matter if the Hembys and Hancocks are related? That has *nothing* to do with tonight." I shook my head.

Hemby High and Hancock High had been rivals for a long time. It made sense that the rivalry started somewhere. We had learned a long time ago that the area had been settled by a Roger and Betty Hemby and that their descendants' names could be spotted on several street signs. One Hemby daughter married a Hancock and that was how Hancock developed. All this history didn't matter to me. I would bet money every city had its own story, not much different than ours. But Silvia wanted me to feel sorry for her because her last name pulled rank over the rest of our stories. She expected too much. I wanted to be at home. Not with her. Not on my way to Owen's rager. Not on my way to face Carlos!

Silvia laughed. The kind of laugh that makes your insides curl. "You really have no idea! The Hembys have to keep proving themselves over and over and over again!" I kept my mouth shut as she added. "My family has been trying to prove, for a very long time, that we are equally worthy of the Hemby legacy. It's all a sick game. Always has been. Always will be."

I was quiet. I didn't want to know more. We drove along the lake and I could see a few lights from houses on the other side of the lake. We passed several large homes with giant garages. I knew we were getting closer to Owen's home because the houses began to look older. Still mansion-like, but bricks and elegant columns were more common.

We pulled up to the largest brick house of them all. It was three stories high, and it had three chimneys. A large porch wrapped around the front half of the house with several large white pillars. It was clearly Owen's house since cars were parked in every parking spot and all along Lake Drive.

Silvia took a deep breath like she was getting ready to be who she needed to be once she got out of my car. It was the first time I had a glimpse into Silvia's world. Yet, I still didn't feel any pity. I still didn't like her. In fact, I was pissed at her for what she had done to Joseph.

I parked between two pickup trucks along Lake Drive, further away from the house than I liked. I walked next to Silvia as we headed toward the loud music. "Thanks for bringing me." Silvia looked sideways at me to see if I was even listening.

I was. "You're welcome." I couldn't smile, but I tried to be less salty. "But you better not get trashed at this party. Because you are too big for me to carry over my shoulder. Remember I *am* your babysitter! And I'm not afraid to tell everyone."

She smirked. "We'll see."

I stopped on the bottom of the steps that led up to the huge porch. Silvia didn't even turn to look at me as she reached the porch and headed right through the front door. It was no big deal for her to flip her popular, partying, homecoming-queen-switch back on.

I sighed and headed up the steps.

Chapter 39

The Rager

"You did come!" Vashon surprised me as I stood in the fancy hallway facing a winding staircase directly in front of me. Vashon was sitting on the bottom three steps, sweet talking some girl I had never seen. Three of his friends claimed several of the steps right above him, each one more interested in their phone than the party. Vashon stood up and walked toward me. The girl just leaned her elbows back onto the step behind her and gave me a full once over. She didn't seem too worried. My dad's jacket was no sexy party dress. "I thought you said you weren't coming."

"It's a long story." I wasn't getting into it again. "But how'd you get here?"

"My granny brought me." He had a huge grin on his face. "And a few of my friends." He pointed at the three boys, who awkwardly waved at me.

"You dragged them along didn't you." I shook my head at him.

Vashon shrugged. "Look. It was the only way Granny would bring me. She's known the Hemby family her whole life, so she knew where to bring me. But she'll be back to pick us up by 9. I didn't dare argue."

I smiled. "Looks like you're having a good time already." I nodded toward the girl who had pulled out her phone.

"I am." He grinned and backed away from me.

I wondered which room I should enter. The one on my left had a huge fireplace. But it was packed with people spread out on several couches and chairs. About five people hung out along the hearth. The base of the fireplace was as deep and wide as a small couch. It looked to me like most of the football team was trying to cram into that room. Most of them faced a huge flat-screen TV that covered a wall. Some movie was streaming. But you couldn't hear a word because of blasting music. No one cared. Cans and bottles were already scattered all over the place.

I spotted Silvia as she came out of a back room with a plate of food in one hand. A six pack of beer was dangling from the other. She walked toward a couple making out on a couch. I couldn't see their faces. But Owen's red hair and Chastity's long, wavy brown hair, told me all I needed to know. As soon as Silvia reached them, she shoved them so they could make room for her. Chastity and Owen laughed at Silvia but shook their heads at the same time. Silvia simply held up the beer. The lovebirds smiled and quickly made room for Silvia to join them.

That was enough for me. I decided to walk into the room to my right instead. I was surprised to see that it had a fireplace with the exact same look as the other one. But the couches and chairs in this room were a little more formal. Fewer people hung out. Maybe because there was no flat-screen to distract them. A few sweet girls I'd grown up with waved at me from their couch. But then they giggled at something they were talking about. Two football players stood near one end of the fireplace and kept gawking at the two girls. I rolled my eyes.

Mateo, from first period, was stretched out in a huge lounge chair in the corner of the room. As always, he had his earbuds in. He glanced at me, but quickly looked back at his phone. I could have sworn I saw him frown. It was strange to see him at this party. But what did I know? This was clearly a very different party than the one I tried to throw.

I headed to the fireplace and claimed a spot at the other end of the hearth. The two awkward boys still had plenty of room at their end of the fireplace to keep staring at the girls. They didn't even look at me, which was okay with me. It didn't take long for the heat from the fire to force me to take off Dad' s jacket.

"Well, hello, sweet momma." I cringed. I hadn't been there for more than ten minutes and I already had to deal with Carlos. I looked directly at him as he stood in front of the swinging door with a plate of food. I did *not* smile or respond. I was thankful there were people in the room with me as he moved closer. He settled on the hearth next to me as Blake swung through the door with his own plate of food. His eyes grew wide when he saw me, but then smiled to cover up whatever thought had crossed his mind. Carlos reached over and tugged on my loose sweatshirt. "You can't hide sexy."

I grabbed my sleeve before it came off my shoulder. "Don't touch me!" I slid over a few inches, but Carlos moved with me.

"You want some food?" Carlos held the plate up to me and pointed at five chicken wings perched on top of a pile of fried rice, and four pieces of pizza. "Careful, the wings are really hot." He nudged my shoulder. "Like you." He smelled like he'd already been drinking.

Blake chuckled nervously. "That's funny. Right, Zonta?" He sat in a chair in front of me.

"No, it's not, Blake." I looked at the blond boy who had become nothing more to me than a symbol of a bully's sidekick. "It is NEVER funny to me. Because I do *not* like Carlos. It doesn't matter how much he likes me or thinks he can win me over by sexually harassing me.

And, he needs to stop." Blake's eyes widened and he nodded at me like he understood what I was saying for the first time.

"I'm sitting right here." Carlos pulled his plate away from me. "Don't talk about me like I'm not here." He quickly got up and stood in front of me, blocking out Blake's face. I didn't want to look at Carlos's thighs, so I looked up at him. He sneered, "I offered you my food and you tell me to back off? That's a low blow." I was a little surprised. Was he really hurt? Was this going to be the end of it? Was he really as pitiful as Ms. Nazari had said? I felt some relief as Carlos shook his head and headed back toward the swinging door. "Come on, Blake, let's get away from this bitch."

The word stung. Bitch. I had never been called that for real, only as a joke or when Vonny teased me. But at that moment the word landed like a rock in the pit of my stomach. I pushed that sick feeling away and I told myself that this had to be good. It had to mean that Carlos would finally leave me alone.

Blake stood up, but before he left, he studied my face for a moment, like he was trying to figure me out. Once Blake was gone, the girls and the awkward guys moved into the other room. We had clearly messed up their mood. I didn't know what to do or where to go, so I stayed next to the fire and gripped Dad's jacket that I had spread across my lap. It was going to be a very long night.

Chapter 40

Mateo

"Why are you here?" someone asked. I turned my head to find Mateo looking at me. We were the last two people still in this room. His whole body stretched across the lounge chair. He pulled his earbuds out of his ears and placed his phone face down on one leg as he stared at me with his dark, piercing eyes.

"What?" I was confused. Mateo never spoke. Or at least never spoke to me. Except when we discussed the 8th Amendment last semester. But talking about the law didn't much count as talking to each other.

"Why. Are. You. Here?" He slowed it down, like I was an idiot.

"Why. Do. You. Care?" I shot back. Not being nice was getting easier.

Mateo stared at me for longer than was comfortable. I stared back. It actually looked like he was calculating if he cared or not. He finally shook his head, frustrated with himself more than anything. "I really don't care." He picked up his phone to ignore me. But, as he began to put his earbuds back in, he stopped and put the phone down. "I guess I do care."

My eyebrows rose. "Really? Why is that?"

Slowly, Mateo removed himself from his chair, clearly fighting his own inner voice telling him to stay seated. It was strange. When he started heading toward me, he sighed. The one part of him had finally given in to the fact that he was going to talk to me whether he wanted to or not. I had to smile. "Is it really so bad to talk to me?"

Mateo plopped down next to me. "It's not that." He sighed again. "You need to leave, Zonta."

"What?" I was trying to read his face, but he wasn't looking at me. He was watching the opening to the hallway, the opening that led to the other room. Then he'd glance over to the swinging door that Carlos and Blake had used only minutes earlier.

"My cousin, Angel Ramirez, is the center on the football team." Mateo stated. He glanced at me, and I shrugged. I sort of knew who that was, but I still didn't know why it mattered. Mateo continued. "My aunt makes me go with him to all these parties because she doesn't trust anyone. Except me. It gets old." He took a deep breath. "Angel tells me everything that the guys on the team talk about. Everything." He rolled his eyes, like it was really a bore. "Anyways,

Carlos was bragging how he was going to hook up with you tonight if you showed up."

I snorted. "Well, that's not happening."

Mateo sighed again. "He said he would hook up with you whether you wanted to or not."

My jaw dropped and that deep burning in my stomach hit me like a rock. I suddenly understood why Blake looked shocked to see me. I felt my breathing change and I started to shake. "But he walked away pissed, like he's over my attitude." I quietly argued.

Mateo turned his head to look straight at me. "Trust me he's not. It's his game." He didn't blink. "You need to leave. The drinking will only make it worse. It will make Carlos lose any ounce of restraint. Which he is already lacking."

I stood up. Panic rising. I promised I would bring Silvia *and* take her home. I needed to leave. I needed to get the hell away from Carlos.

Chapter 41

The Plan

We made a plan to ruin Carlos's sick game he was playing. I pulled in Vashon to help Mateo and me, and he was happy to do his part. It was very simple, really. I stayed in the same room with Mateo as people came and went. I sat on the edge of the small couch closest to his lounge chair, as he listened to music on his phone. Both of us pretended to ignore each other, pretended to be better than the lame party. People left us alone. We were clearly a bore. As soon as 9 p.m. rolled around, I walked into the crowded room with Mateo standing in the hallway watching me. I handed Silvia my car keys and told her I wasn't feeling well. She could drive herself home. I didn't care if she crashed my car or never made it home that night. I was done babysitting.

Mrs. Wilkes, Vashon's granny, was more than happy to give me a ride home. Her white-streaked hair was in a perfect updo, and she was snuggly zipped up in an elegant purple bathrobe. She didn't know me, but I had heard a lot about her. How her words broke through Ozzie's thick skull and kept him from taking those pills. How she was the force that kept Hall a respected and thriving community. I had no worries hopping into her car. She looked me straight in the eyes and could see my relief. She smiled at me and then looked up and touched the plush roof of her car. "I knew the Good Lord was telling me to let my boy come to this party. I couldn't figure it at the time. Now I know why." And that was all she said to me. It was enough.

Vashon looked back at me from the front seat and smiled. "Looks like you did help me get to the party after all." Then he turned to his granny and filled her in on the details.

I couldn't help but laugh. I never thought I would feel so relieved to sit squished between three freshman boys in the back seat of an old Crown Victoria.

The last thing I saw as we pulled away from the driveway, was Mateo as he headed back in to the Hembys' house. I smiled at the thought of him plugging in his earbuds as he reclaimed the lounge chair. I had learned something about Mateo. I was pretty sure he'd sit there all night. He'd do what he had to do to babysit his cousin, the center for the football team.

Chapter 42

Home

I don't know what Mrs. Wilkes told Mom after she pulled up into our drive. I didn't wait to find out. I walked right past Mom, who was standing in the front door with her hand over her mouth. It must have been a sight watching me crawl out of the back of the old car crammed with boys. Then there was Mrs. Wilkes who had also climbed out of the car. She had made sure her bathrobe was zipped up all the way after she let it fall its full length to the ground. She had looked like a queen as she held her head high and had walked me up the driveway.

I flung Dad's jacket into the closet and headed down the hall. The last thing I heard was Mom asking if my car and Silvia were okay. I knew Mrs. Wilkes would set her straight. She did.

I took a long shower. By the time I crawled into bed, Mrs. Wilkes and the boys were gone. As I began to fall asleep, I heard the muffled sounds of Mom and Dad arguing. I took a deep breath and fell asleep knowing that Mom *finally* understood my side.

Chapter 43

Intense

Saturday was intense. My Mom was weepy and she told me she was so sorry, so many times. Part of me felt sorry for her, but the greater part of me did not. I didn't know what Mrs. Wilkes said, but I suspected part of Mom's childhood, growing up in a strong all-black home, came flooding back. Both my parents assured me they would call Ms. Nazari first thing on Monday and tell her they expected Carlos to stay the hell away from me or they would call the law. I rolled my eyes at that. He hadn't really done much except harass me. What could the law do? If word got out, it would just piss Carlos off more. I hoped the school would be quiet about whatever my parents said. I didn't want to deal with even more drama.

Dad poked his head through my door to check on me at least three times before lunch. The fourth time was enough. I pulled off my headphones and looked at him. "I'm fine! Stop checking on me. Nothing happened."

Dad walked through the door and sat down on the floor with me. I had spread out all my SAT study material and was trying to make sense of my notes before I met with Joseph again Tuesday. I had also thrown my U.S. History folder into the mess. We had a test on Monday, and I still needed to study for that too. But I really didn't feel like it. Dad took a deep breath and handed me my car keys. "Silvia just dropped off your car. Pretty sure that she's hungover. Bad."

"Good." I threw the keys onto my pile of shoes.

"Not my worry." He smiled at me. "I want you to know I'm proud of you."

"Dad, you're making this weird." I hated it when Dad talked to me about this stuff. It was just too . . . icky.

He leaned to one side as he tilted his head. "I know. But you need to hear it . . . No . . . I need to say it." He dropped his head for a second. I was secretly praying he wouldn't start crying. I was relieved when he looked back up at me with a huge grin. "I am just so darn proud I have a daughter that's a fighter."

I shook my head. "Dad, I did NOT fight him." I didn't want to go over the whole scenario again. Ever.

He nodded. "Yes, I know. But you would if you had to." We locked eyes for a moment, as I thought about his words. Then I simply nodded. I would. Satisfied, he jumped up and headed for my door. He turned around one last time and added, "Let's hope we never have to find out."

Chapter 44

Time

By Sunday afternoon I'd had enough of my parents. They were trying to act normal, but it was like they had no clue what that looked like anymore. They were too worried. Too sweet. Too clingy. Too much! I had to get out. I wished I was close enough friends with Joseph to hang out with him. But I knew I needed to wait until Tuesday. If I called him before then, he might think I liked him. Which I did. But I didn't want to scare him away.

In the past, I would have scooted over to Vonny's house. But Vonny was still gone and texting her was just not the same. I didn't know Mary Ann well enough yet to ask her if I could pop in. But it felt like we were slowly getting there. I smiled at the thought of Mary Ann, Summer, and Imani all hanging out together . . . with me. It would be fun. Maybe I would ask them next week at lunch.

I had just spent a huge amount of time with Ozzie and didn't want to hang out with him again, yet. I smiled at how easy it was to move into a friendship with him. Then there was what he said about Lilly. I wondered if she would be able to move on too. But I hadn't even tried with her. At least not very hard. Suddenly, I knew where to go. If what Ozzie said was true about Lilly, then she was just waiting for me to step up. Memories of Christmas came flooding back. I felt so guilty. I knew Lilly left because of me. I still hadn't done anything about it. It was about time I did.

I grabbed my Adidas and pulled my car keys out of one of them before I put them on. With one arm holding my U.S. History folder, laptop, and my keys, I headed to the kitchen. I stared at the small kitchen bulletin board and found what I was looking for. Lilly's address. Dad had not moved it since he pinned it there after he talked to the police officer. The same day they found Lilly. I entered the details into my phone. 208 Maple Road.

"Where are you going?" Mom yelled from the living room.

"Out." I didn't really want them to get mental about my plan. Or worse, decide to go with me.

Mom didn't like my answer, so she hurried into the kitchen. "Zonta. After Friday you really think *out* is enough?"

"Mom, I just need space," I explained.

"Why can't you tell me?" She looked all worried. "Do you not trust me any—"

"Mom! Of course I trust you." I had to think. I remembered the folder I was gripping. "I have a history test tomorrow and need to study with a friend from class." It wasn't a lie. She looked at my folder and then relaxed.

"Okay, great. Be safe." She started to walk back into the living room.

"Mom?" I needed one more thing.

She stopped and turned around. "Yes?"

"Can I take the leftover Christmas cookies you froze?"

Mom frowned. "But I was saving them in case Lilly came back. They were her favorites."

"I know. But I'm pretty sure she's not coming back. Might as well not let them get freezer burn."

Mom slowly nodded. "I guess you're right. I do need to let them go. I don't want to waste them. Take them before I change my mind."

I grabbed the large plastic box of cookies out of the freezer and headed out the door. I hoped that Lilly was home. But most of all, I hoped she would be okay with me showing up.

Chapter 45
208 Maple Road

I let my GPS guide me along streets I hadn't driven on in a long time. Bence Avenue turned into 2nd Street, the most direct route into downtown. But instead of heading north on Park Avenue, the GPS guided me one block over and had me head north on Central Avenue. Once I passed the familiar courthouse, it wasn't long before Beck's Bowling came into view on my left. I hadn't been bowling since I was a kid. Across the street still stood the old video store. A huge V was the only letter still attached to the empty building. In spite of the eyesore, Hancock Pizza was on the next corner and their delivery cars were already pulling out of the parking lot with orders.

It was another six blocks or so before I hit 17th Street. I knew 17th street well since Hancock High was only a few blocks down on my right. Pizza World, Hancock Burgers, and a couple of coffee places were hangouts after school.

Only two blocks later, I turned left onto 19th street. Within a minute I turned right onto Maple Road. Her house was on the corner. I parked on the road and stared out my window at the house across from me. I felt my heart race. Was I stupid to think she would even want to talk to me?

I got out of the car and carried my laptop, folder, and the box of cookies up two wooden steps onto a small front porch that was leaning heavily to one side. I didn't see a doorbell so I knocked. When I didn't hear anything, I knocked again. Harder. Still nothing. I felt so stupid as I headed back down the steps. How could I even think she might be home?

Suddenly the door opened behind me. "Zonta?"

I turned around. Lilly was standing there in some sweats and a T-shirt with her hair in a massive mess. She had clearly been sleeping. "Looks like I woke you up. Sorry."

"What are you doing here?" She walked out onto the porch in her bare feet and cracked the door behind her. I could barely see her eyes in the dark, but her body language told me she was chill.

"I thought maybe we could study for our history test together." Then I held up the box of cookies. "Brought snacks too!" I walked back to the porch. "But, if you can't, I get it. But you can have these." I handed her the cookies.

Lilly opened the box and laughed. "Seriously?" She held up a sugar cookie covered in green icing and sprinkles. "Are these what I think they are?"

I shrugged. "I'm afraid so. Mom froze them, so when you came back you could have them." I smiled. "She's just a little too much sometimes."

Lilly smiled. "Yes. But lucky me." She held the cookie in her mouth while she shoved the lid back on the box. Then she proceeded to chomp into the cookie. "Still good . . . even a little frozen." I saw Lilly shiver.

"Aren't you cold?" I pointed out the obvious. "Should we go inside?"

Lilly swallowed her bite and looked at me. "Not so sure you'll like my place."

"Sure, I will." I smiled. How bad could it be?

"Nope. Not true." She took another bite and started shivering without stopping.

"It doesn't matter what I think of where you live. I just want to know if you want to study with me or not?" I held up my laptop and folder. "I am serious about studying."

Lilly took a deep breath. "Okay. Come in. But I swear, not one word!"

"I promise."

Chapter 46

What?

I walked into the dark house with Lilly right behind me. The smell hit me first. It was a sour musty smell. But I didn't say anything. As the door closed behind me Lilly flipped on the light. I could finally see her wild green eyes and they weren't glaring at me. I wanted to keep it that way, so I made sure I didn't even look like the smell bothered me.

Clearly, she'd been sleeping on the couch that was a few feet away from us. A pillow and a few blankets were inviting her to come snuggle back under them. Which she did. It didn't take long for her to stop shivering. A table and two chairs were shoved up against a wall with several random items piled on them. Clearly, they were used for storage and not for eating meals. An old green fridge and a matching oven stood on opposites sides of a small sink and countertop. The only thing separating the kitchen from the living room was a small strip of linoleum that started where the wood floor stopped.

"Where's your room?" I asked. "Maybe we should study in there. Don't want to disturb your aunt."

Lilly laughed. "She's gone to work. For a change. And . . ." She pointed at the couch. "*This* is my bedroom." I couldn't hide my surprise. Then I took a second to look at the items on the table. They were all of Lilly's clothes, neatly stacked, and her green camo backpack. When I didn't say anything, she shook her head. "Told you that you wouldn't like it."

Without thinking I said, "You know you still have a room at our house." Then I grabbed my mouth. "No. I didn't mean to say that. Sorry."

Lilly laughed at me and then opened the cookie box again. As she helped herself to her second cookie she explained, "Yes, you did mean that, and Monta wouldn't mind having me back either." She took a bite. "I do miss her cooking!"

"Dad too!" I added, not caring for the first time that she called my mother by her first name.

"Yes, Zeb too!" She smiled. "Look, Zonta. It's all good here. Even if it looks bad to you. My aunt is getting her life together and her boyfriend still hasn't dared to come back again." She patted her covers. "And this couch is more comfortable than you think."

I nodded and opened the folder. "Okay, great. Ready to study?" Lilly nodded. But right before I went over the first study question, I looked at her again. "I just have one more thing to say."

"About my house?" Lilly teased.

I smiled, but then it faded. "No. I just wanted to say I was . . . I mean . . . I *am* sorry about chasing you away."

Lilly stared at me. It was strange. It was like she was putting together a puzzle in her head. "What? You think I left because of *you*?"

My mouth dropped. "What? Didn't you? I thought you were pissed at me."

"For not checking on me, stupid!" Lilly knocked the cookie box into my arm.

At that moment I stared at her. Nothing made sense. "I don't get it."

Lilly opened the box of cookies again and, this time, offered me one. I grabbed one with white icing. "Look. Remember the phone your parents tried to give me as a gift?"

"Yeah." I took a bite. It was still half frozen, and Lilly was right. It tasted great.

"You see, if I had taken the phone then it would have become a huge problem." She looked at me clearly trying to find the words to best explain it. "Zonta, I've been taking care of myself for so long. Having Zeb and Monta suddenly want to manage and control my life would have been awful."

"But they would never control you." I still didn't understand.

Lilly pulled out her third cookie. "It's hard for you to understand because you've never been completely in charge of your own life. I mean every bit of it. Food, clothes, where you sleep. *Everything*."

"But isn't that a problem?" I asked. "Don't you want all those things? Don't you want to stop worrying about those things?"

"I do. But . . . not if I owe others at the same time. And not if I can't make my own choices anymore," she explained.

"But my parents would never feel that way."

"They may not, but I would always feel like I owed them." Lilly took a bite of her cookie before she added, "And worse, I would start fighting them if they started making adult decisions for me." She looked right at me. "You see, Zonta. Once you've become an adult, there is no going back to being a child."

I wasn't about to argue that Lilly was more a child than an adult in my eyes. I realized there was so much about Lilly's life that I didn't understand. Not because I didn't want to, but because I did *not* live her life. "Okay." I smiled. "But maybe coming over for dinner once in a while wouldn't hurt your adult self!"

Lilly smiled. "With Monta's cooking, you don't have to ask me twice."

We spent the next two hours studying and talking. I told her about the rager and what Mateo and Vashon did for me. She listened to every word. THEN I told her about Joseph, which got us off topic completely. By the time I left, I felt lighter. I had totally misread Lilly. A mistake I didn't want to make again.

Chapter 47

Alone

Mateo nodded to me as I walked into first period Monday morning. I nodded back. A small smile spread across my face, but he looked away before his *self-that-cared* had to return the smile. I saw Lilly catch the whole exchange and she raised her eyebrows and smiled. I was glad I had told her the whole story the day before at her house. When I had gotten home, I told my parents where I had been, and they were thrilled that Lilly would come have dinner with us sometime. That Monday morning, I gave her a *we'll-talk more-later* look. She smiled and went back to staring at everyone else walking through the door.

Emma Tang-Lee was at her desk ignoring the rest of us. I wondered what Joseph was doing at that moment. Probably in one of his classes at Hemby University. I looked forward to our next tutoring session.

As Ms. Williams started class I glanced over at Ozzie's desk. It was still empty. But on Wednesday he would be back. His calming presence would be welcome. I glanced to the back of the room and realized I hadn't seen Carlos or Blake that morning. My whole body felt relief. This would be a great Monday. Maybe even a great week.

I was ready for my U.S. History test, thanks to studying with Lilly. But, about 40 minutes into class, I had to go to the bathroom. I had downed a huge cup of coffee that morning, more than usual. I excused myself and headed down the hall, past my locker into the girls' bathroom. Just as I was finishing up, I heard someone slam the door hard as they entered the girl's bathroom. I wondered who was already pissed that early in the morning.

"Zonta!" Carlos yelled. "I know you're in here."

I felt myself freeze. My heart raced and my stomach burned. I didn't answer. I had to think.

"You think you can threaten me? How dare you tell the school you'll call the police!" He slammed each stall door open. They were all empty. I was alone.

Chapter 48

Attack

I felt so stupid. My parents must have talked to Ms. Nazari early enough that they grabbed Carlos and Blake first thing. They weren't absent. They were in the office. Being warned.

I quickly stood up so I could pull up my pants. I almost had them zipped when my door flung open. Carlos stood there staring at me. "Get out of here, Carlos!" I said firmly.

He didn't say anything. He was done talking. His eyes were fierce, and his black hair fell halfway across his face as he stepped into the stall with me. He tried to move in to kiss me, but I lifted a knee to try and kick him. But he was faster, shoving it back down with one hand. He then grabbed a handful of my hair to hold back my head. His other hand reached for my half-way-zipped-up pants and tried to pull them down. Panic set in as I felt his body move in. I had to think. Suddenly, I remembered Ozzie's words *scream sooner and louder and keep hitting him in every place that would hurt.*

And that's what I did. I screamed and flung my hands at every part of his body I could reach. I couldn't reach his eyes, but I managed to swing one hand so hard that it hit his right ear. He groaned and let go of my head to hold his ear, so I tried to move past him. But his other hand still gripped my pants. "Not so fast."

"Carlos. Stop it!" Blake was suddenly standing in front of the sinks.

"Shut up, Blake!" Carlos yelled. "Go stand at the door and tell me if someone's coming. I'm going to teach this bitch a lesson."

I didn't wait for them to make any more plans. I screamed again and came at Carlos's ear again. This time he let go of my pants and used both his hands to hold down my arms. He dragged me out of the stall and flung me to the floor. His body came down with mine so he could straddle me. Once he had me pinned using his legs, he tried to cover my screaming mouth. I bit his hand, which caused him to slap me.

Suddenly, it felt as if Carlos was lighter. He was moving away from me. Confused he yelled, "Blake! What the—"

"I SAID STOP IT!" Blake's voice was fierce. As quick as lighting one of Carlos's legs was lifted away by a very pale arm. At the same time, Blake's other arm snaked around Carlos's neck and reached down to clasp the arm that was still bringing the knee closer to Carlos's face. His right arm was pinned in between Blake's two hands now firmly clasped together across Carlos's chest. The intense hold from behind caused Carlos to try and stand with the one free leg, but, instead, he and Blake quickly fell backwards onto the bathroom tiles. With a strength I had never seen before, Blake held Carlos in place. I quickly sat up and scooted toward the back wall. My heart was racing, but I was finally able to zip up my pants.

As I faced the boys again, I saw Blake still had Carlos in the same grip. When Carlos could barely move, he resorted to cussing up a storm. With his one free arm, he scratched Blake's left forearm until it bled. It was just enough time for Mr. Soza and two teachers to reach us. The janitor quickly helped Blake subdue Carlos while other adults and teens began to pour into the bathroom. Many were quickly told to leave. But not before they had taken in the whole scene.

Within minutes the police arrived and took Carlos out in cuffs. Ms. Nazari fell to her knees in front of me and told me to stay put until EMS checked me out. I obeyed. But I did ask her one question. "Do you believe me now?"

Ms. Nazari patted my arm as she nodded her head. She leaned in and whispered. "I will fix this. Trust me!" I didn't trust her. How could I? She hadn't believed me before. I was thankful when someone called her name. The last thing I needed was to make sure she felt good about herself. Ms. Nazari gave me one last look. "I mean it!" Then she quickly stood up and walked over to talk to a police officer.

My whole body was sore. I didn't know if I should cry or scream as the attack played over and over in my head. Then I remembered Blake. I looked over at him and saw blood dripping from his left forearm. He smiled awkwardly at me and said, "I may suck at football, but I'm pretty good at wrestling."

Chapter 49

Changed

I couldn't even respond to Blake. I didn't know what to think or what I should feel. As I started to focus in on the flurry of activity in front of me, I realized that not all of the students were following Mr. Soza's directions to leave. Mateo's face appeared first as he pushed his way through the wave of teens trying to exit. He stopped in front of me and shook his head, fire in his eyes. He looked over at Blake, still propped up against the bathroom wall waiting for EMS, and headed toward him. Mateo's glare told me all I needed to know. It would not end well for Blake.

I reached out my hand and grabbed Mateo's ankle. "Mateo, wait! Blake stopped Carlos. He helped me!" Mateo looked down at me and then back at Blake who was wide-eyed and nodding.

"Yes, I did. I sure did." He repeated several times until Mateo stepped back in my direction.

Suddenly, Emma Tang-Lee's face appeared in the small crowd behind Mr. Soza's arm. Confusion flickered across her face as she took in the scene. Emma frowned as she looked at Blake and then at me. There was a lot she would have to figure out too. Then as quickly as she had appeared she was gone, along with most of the gawking students.

But Lilly did not pay attention to anyone telling her to move on. No, not Lilly. She flung her arms around and raised her voice until Mr. Soza gave up and let her through. I looked up at Lilly, standing there in her blue sweater. She continued to ignore everyone around her as she plopped down next to me. I whispered, "What did you say to Mr. Soza?"

"Really?" Lilly pushed the hair out of my face. "That's what's on your mind?" I shrugged, but then flinched. My whole body hurt. Lilly scooted in even closer and leaned into me. "I told him that he better let me through, or he'd have your parents to deal with."

I tried to smile. "I guess you used your adult voice?"

"I sure did," she whispered. "I'll teach you sometime."

As Lilly continued to try to clean me up a little, I realized that Mateo was still standing between Blake and me. He also continued to scan the bathroom. What else could possibly happen? It didn't matter, really. I was not so sure what made Mateo decide to care, but whatever it was, I was thankful for it.

I looked over at Blake who was taking it all in. He'd glance up at Mateo and then over at Lilly and me. Then, he would take a few minutes to stare at the ceiling. He repeated this several times, and once in a while he'd check his bloody arm. For the first time, I felt something for Blake. I was not only in awe for what he had done for me or for what he had risked. But I also felt happy for him and sorry for him at the same time. The old Blake that I thought I knew was not sitting on the girls' bathroom floor across from me. Something had changed.

I wanted to let him know that I had changed too. But I was still very much in a daze and gave up trying to worry about Blake. I'd talk to him when I was ready.

Mateo remained standing near me, like a protective wall. Lilly had no problem waiting on the nasty floor with me. Suddenly, the shock of what had happened hit me and I began to shake. Lilly shoved a strand of my hair behind my ears and straightened up my shirt that was hanging off one shoulder. Then she pulled off her blue sweater and wrapped it around me. "You'll be alright. I promise."

It was hard to believe her at that moment. But after all she had been through, she was still standing. Maybe I would too.

I leaned my head on her shoulder as we sat there together waiting for EMS.

Acknowledgements

Writing *Zonta* could never have happened without the help of several individuals. A special thanks to all of the following people who played a role in the process. I am forever grateful to each of you for the time and support you provided. Your engagement in the story and responses to the characters inspire me to continue on this journey into the world of Hancock High.

To my parents Jonlyn and G. Keith Parker, who were willing to take on the first read-through of the manuscript *and* multiple additional drafts. They have not only embraced the characters' lives with gusto, but they have shown unwavering support for the whole writing process. To Ben Onachila, who also was willing to take on the first read-through and provide me with refreshing feedback. His uncanny poetic ability has helped me iron out some rough edges. To my daughters, Maya Borhaug and Sarah Borhaug, whose read-throughs helped me keep the story and characters real. To Kym Sebranek, Sheila Mooney, Jennifer Sensabaugh, Jose Rene Perez, Michael Bower, Shutao Wang, Mary Ann Galyon and Dr. Tara P. Bacote for reading through the manuscript and providing valuable feedback, each bringing their unique perspective to the table, supporting my desire to provide an authentic story. To Nastia Parker for not only reading through the manuscript but guiding me through the intricate world of social media and texting trends.

Brevard North Carolina's former Police Chief, Phil Harris, for details on police procedure and terminology and Elijah Eubanks for reviewing over wrestling references. Thank you to Beth Branagan, school social worker, for her insight into teen homelessness.

Olivia Lytle for her willingness to model for the cover and read through the manuscript. My daughter, Amy Borhaug, who whispers words of perseverance and courage. Nioca Robinson, whose encouragement I dearly value.

My copy editor Julie Overpeck, who not only understands the importance of Hi-Lo books, but helped turn out a professional product.

A special thanks to Transylvania County Schools and Brevard High School for the use of their property for the cover shot.

Sarah Borhaug's time, commitment, creativity and professional skill in shooting, editing and designing the cover are deeply appreciated.

Last but not least, my husband, Tore, for his unwavering support and his steady grounding. Without him, none of it would be possible.

Zonta's Text/Slang/Terms

The following are definitions for terms used in *Zonta*. Some terms may have other definitions that are not included in this mini-glossary.

2—to, too, two

abt—about

b—be

bf—boyfriend

cmon—come on

fab—fabulous

groovy—excellent/wonderful

hw—homework

idk—I don't know

lava lamp—a glass structure that is filled with liquid and wax that are heated, which causes the wax to float around, creating different shapes

linoleum—type of flooring made out of natural materials

lol—laugh out loud

nw—no way

omg—oh my gosh/God/goodness

Picasso—Pablo Picasso was a famous artist who lived from 1881 to 1973 who was known for his abstract art

plz—please

r—are

rager—big party

rmbr—remember

rn—right now

pic—picture

SAT—a test used by colleges/universities to measure how ready a student is for college/university. Used to compare students. This is often one factor used to help decide who should be admitted.

sick—1. awful 2. awesome/cool

tbh—to be honest

thnx—thanks

tmi—too much information

ttyl—talk to you later

u—you

updo—hairstyle that is up and away from the face

vibes—feeling/mood

vinyl—a synthetic/artificial material, a type of plastic

w/—with

y—why?